Jade

Joseph R. Lallo

Dedication

Jade was written as a linker to a story that I've yet to publish, and was published before the end of the story it was intended to follow. This is dedicated to the readers who have stuck with me despite my utterly nonsensical publishing decisions.

Acknowledgements

I would like to acknowledge my editor Anna Genoese and, as always, my cover artist Nick Deligaris.

Chapter 1

A man laid on the forest floor, weak, air dragging in and out of his lungs in fading gasps. Already his vision was growing dim. He was beyond help now. The end was near.

A dying mind must choose its thoughts carefully. They are too precious to be squandered.

He thought of his family--his wife, his brothers, his parents, each and every one of them waiting on the other side. He would be with them again soon. He thought of how little he was leaving behind. A tiny home, a failure of a shop, and an indifferent town. He would not miss them. Still a young man, he thought of the years of life that he was losing. Half of a lifetime still lay before him. He would not miss that, either. The world he knew was a bleak one. Disease, hunger, and poverty were everywhere. What he felt most was relief that he would endure it no more.

Most impressively, not once did his final thoughts touch upon the beast standing over him. Blood pooled around its mighty claws. A cold rain began to pound upon its green scales. Its reptilian head towered above, smoky breath rushing out between stout daggers of teeth. The dragon watched life slip away, just as it had countless times before. Then, in a few bounding strides, it was gone.

#

"All out! Everybody out!" cried a scraggly man, as he hammered at a crude bell.

Far to the southeast, the town of Isintist was a small one, but dense with people. They poured from the houses as quickly as they could. It was the alarm bell, and the smell of smoke left little doubt as to the reason. A fire was raging in a large house toward the edge of town, the site of the Rinton family's home and farm. Every able body rushed to the scene. It would be nice to say that each had moved so quickly out of a sense of duty, but the truth was far less heroic. The village--indeed, the entire region--was in the midst of a terrible drought. The grass and trees were dry as tinder. Were the fire to spread, it would quickly be out of control and their own homes would be next. Best, then, to do what could be done to stop it before that happened.

The burning home was already surrounded by onlookers, but there was little anyone could do. The whole of the lower floor was utterly engulfed. Even if a would-be hero were to brave the burning doorway, there was no hope of rescuing anyone inside. With the wells all but dry, neither was there any hope to douse the flames. And so the town was left to helplessly watch as flames worked their way up to the attic. The intensity of the inferno devoured the supports of the building, causing charred lower walls to creak and splinter under what little remained untouched above.

Finally, in a rush of embers and debris, the foremost section of the attic tumbled forward. An instant before it struck the ground, a form tumbled from its window, colliding viciously with the ground and rolling toward the crowd. The rest of the house, finally having reached its breaking point, collapsed. A scalding hot rush of air erupted from it, filling the surrounding field with smoke, ash, and splintered wood. The assembled townsfolk scattered to beat out the dozens of smaller fires started by the flying embers--but, for some, the sound of cries of anguish and pain drew their attention to the ground in front of the smoldering remains of the attic loft.

There, just beyond the mound of broken and shattered wood, was a little girl, not more than six years old. The collapse had spared her, and though the fall from the window and the choking smoke hadn't done her any good, she was alive, the only survivor of the terrible disaster.

When the flames died away, there were questions to be answered. In an ideal world, there would have been questions about the nature of the disaster. How did the fire start? Why was the whole of the family inside during the day? How could the fire have spread so quickly that not a single one of the five Rinton family members could reach a door?

Alas, this was a simple time, and curiosity was hardly a common virtue. The fire was never presumed to be anything more than a terrible tragedy. Thus, the only questions left to be answered were what to do with the land, and what to do with the girl. In a community so small and so remote, there was seldom any need for laws more complex than an eye for an eye, so the matter was one with no clear resolution. To address it, a meeting of the town leaders was called. The most influential people in town, and anyone else with any interest, gathered in the church for the informal meeting. When all were ready, it was called to order.

"Right, so, by now we all heard the terrible news about the Rintons," announced an old man to a general murmur of acknowledgment.

The old man's name was Delnick, and he was the unofficial leader of the town largely because he'd managed to stay alive for so long. A lifetime in the sun had made him look as though he'd been stitched together from tanned cowhide, but his mind still seemed sharp, and since no one else wanted the job, no one challenged his authority.

"So what are we going to do about all that land?" asked a man in the rear of the room.

The man turned out to be a fellow named Drudder. He was known around town primarily for his bitter attitude and ruinous gambling habit.

"Little Jade survived the fire, so the land belongs to her," Delnick proclaimed.

"What!? She can't tend to that land! That land'll be wasted if you give it to her!" He objected.

"Look, the girl gets the land. We ain't discussing it. Of course she can't tend to it! She's not even six yet. We need to find her a place to live," said Delnick. "Now, who can look after her until we can find a family member to take her?"

There was a low murmur again, but no volunteers. The drought had hit the village hard. Most had difficulty turning up enough food and water for their own families. Supporting another was more than any of the residents could handle.

"I'll take her," said Drudder. "I got three boys already, what's one more? And, naturally I'll work the land on her behalf."

Delnick sat in silent consideration for a few moments. No one was foolish enough to believe that Drudder had the girl's best interests at heart. He just wanted the Rinton land, which was some of the most fertile in the region. That didn't change the fact that no one else had offered, and the girl needed a home.

"All right, Drudder. Watch the girl and the land is yours until we find a next of kin," he said.

A little girl, eyes still red from smoke and tears, was led by her hand to her new guardian.

"Th-thank you, Mr. Dru--" she began meekly.

"Gale! Take the Rinton girl back home and set her up in the boys' room. I've got to head over to the land and make sure the fire didn't do anything to the fence," Drudder cried to his weary-looking wife.

And so Jade's new life began. By day, she walked past the charred remains of her former home to work the land that had belonged to her parents. She pulled weeds, planted seeds, and did anything else her new guardian asked of her. She did it well, too. The land she worked sprouted twice as many green shoots as that worked by the others. Work continued until the sun was slipping from the sky. By night, she sat in a sad daze in the corner of a room crowded with three boys at least twice her age.

To say that the Drudders were cruel to her would be a lie. They never truly mistreated her. Nor could one say that they failed to provide for her. There was a roof over her head, and even a bed of her own. The drought meant that the food on the table was barely enough, but she always got an equal share. No, her new family gave her everything that they had to give her . . . and that was all. Her "brothers" barely glanced in her direction. Her "father" spoke only in directions regarding this task or that in the fields. She was never called by any name other than "Rinton girl," or more often simply "you there." For a girl so young, a girl who had lost her family so horribly and so quickly, the loneliness was pure agony.

Before long, Jade was reduced to wandering numbly through her day, quietly doing as she was told, eating her meager meals, and sleeping fitfully. She was in just such a daze, weeding the edge of the family land nearest to the trees, when she felt something. For a moment, it cut through the veil of malaise.

It wasn't that she had seen something, or even heard something. There was simply a sensation . . . like something in the trees was watching her. She squinted into the sparse, dried out woods, but it was no use. The bright sun made the relative shade of the woods a veritable wall of darkness. Still, she could not shake the feeling. Moving slowly, she squeezed through the fence and crept closer to the trees. Her eyes began to adjust, cutting deeper into the shade. There was something there . . .

In an explosion of motion, a frightened deer burst from the trees and ran off along the fence. Startled, Jade squealed and fell backward. Her eyes, tearing up from the shock of the creature's appearance, first watched it gallop away, then turned to the forest again. There was still something there. She couldn't make out what it was, but it was big, and it was moving.

For the moment, her curiosity managed to drown out the voices of both reason and fear. Whatever the beast in the forest was, it was moving very quietly. Jade could make out its form, but no details. It just seemed like a mass of green moving deeper into the forest. She crept forward, but with each step she took toward it, the shape retreated faster, until finally it was out of sight. Jade squinted after it, but there was no question, it was gone. She looked around her. Here and there branches and bushes seemed snapped away. Then she looked down. There, on the parched forest floor, was a footprint. It was huge, and looked almost like the sort a rooster might leave behind if it were the size of an elephant. Just as the wheels in her young mind began to turn, and fear began to trickle back into place, a gruff voice rang out.

"Girl! Where have you run off to?" called Drudder.

Jade hurried back to the light of the field and spent the rest of the day trying not to think about what she had seen. As is so often the case, those things we wish to forget have a terrible habit of consuming our minds. She tried to work the land. She tried to eat her meal. Every moment, her young mind was churning on the images she'd seen. The conclusion was obvious, but too terrifying to consider. Finally, just as the empty plates were being cleared away, the words that she'd tried so dutifully to keep from her mind found their way to her mouth.

"I saw a dragon," she said quietly.

The silence came slowly. Curious eyes turned in her direction; her adoptive family reacted roughly as they would have if a piece of furniture had made the comment.

"Did you say a dragon?" asked one of the boys.

"You didn't see a dragon," said Drudder.

"I did, it was in the forest next to--"

"You didn't see a dragon!" he repeated firmly.

"Dragons live in the mountains; we're in the plains," said the youngest brother.

"Everybody would have seen it if there was a dragon here," said the middle boy.

"Everybody would be dead if there was a dragon here," said the eldest.

"Don't make up stories," Drudder advised.

"But I--"

"Don't," he repeated firmly.

Jade sheepishly closed her mouth and lowered her eyes. From that day onward, she did not say a word to anyone about what she had seen, but the edge of the fields nearest to the forest went suspiciously unweeded.

The days without rain continued to tick by, and one by one the wells began to run dry. The only water that remained came in the trickle of a stream that grew weaker by the day. Despair was steadily turning to desperation as the people fought for every drop of water to keep first their crops, then themselves, from withering away. When finally even the stream was little more than a dry bed, a meeting was once again called of the town leaders.

"It ain't natural. It just ain't natural," raved Drudder.

"I'll agree with you there, Drudder," said Delnick, "but knowing it ain't natural doesn't do us much good, does it?"

"Well, what could cause a drought this bad?"

"Any number of things. There could be a witch or a wizard. The Gods could be mad at us. Some sort of mystic beast could be bringing it down on us. We could be cursed . . ." Delnick considered.

"Hold it . . . hold it . . . Could a dragon do this?" Drudder asked, the little girl's words echoing in his mind.

"Yeah . . . Yeah, a dragon could. Course a dragon could. Dragons can do damn near anything," replied Delnick, in the distinctive tone of growing certainty shared by all supposed leaders when confronted with something they are unsure of. "But if there was a dragon about, someone would have seen it."

"The Rinton girl saw one, weeks back. I figured she was just imagining things."

"Well, we've gotta be sure. You boys head home and arm yourselves. We need to find out if there is a dragon around here," Delnick quickly ordered. There were already plenty of people whispering doubts of the old man's ability to lead. Now that there was a direction, best to start moving immediately. "If there is, at least we know why we're in such a bad state. Go, now!"

Hesitantly, the most able men the town had to offer set about the task. Starting with the forest where Jade had first seen the beast, they searched. Slowly but surely, the clues began to arise. Here and there, a half-hidden footprint that no beast in the area should have been able to leave would be found. Then came the partially buried remains of a charred stag. Finally, some distance out of town, a shallow cave leading into the sandy ground bore a smell unmistakable to Kruck, the one and only man in town who had encountered a dragon before. The men gathered again to discuss their findings. The fact that Kruck waved a hook in place of a hand while he spoke added significant weight to his words.

"You're dealing with one of the fire-breathing devils, all right. Down in Teller's Pit. It is a smart one, too, or someone is trying to cover for it. It tries to wipe up its tracks, and it tries to hide its kills. Gods willing we won't ever *see* this thing, but I can tell you that it is damn sure here," Kruck raved.

"And as long as that thing is here, this drought will continue . . ." Delnick surmised, "What will it take to kill it?"

"More than we got, that's for sure," Kruck replied, "You don't want to fight the thing, anyway. That'll just make it angry. We should all just be glad it hasn't attacked *us* . . . yet."

All eyes turned to Delnick. He stroked his chin.

"I want all of you to go back to your homes. I'll think of something . . . and if any of you have an idea, you share it with me . . . Until then, we'll just hope that whatever has kept that monster from killing us with fire instead of drying us out will keep doing it. Just try to pretend you aren't living with a dragon breathing down your necks."

With that less than sage plan, life in the town of Isintist continued, such as it was. Days passed with no solution, each of the townspeople nervously working in the shadow of the monster. Drudder leaned upon his hoe and peered over the half-tilled field. The land stretched all the way to the trees and, impossibly, it was fruitful. It was anything but a bountiful crop, but scattered patches of land had managed to produce wheat. He looked over the spotty green stretches, vaguely recalling that each had been worked by Jade . . . As a matter of fact, only those worked by Jade seemed to grow. He set the thought aside. It must have been the land. It was nothing like his own. Last year's harvest, in a year that had seen plenty of rain, had barely been enough to survive on, let alone cover his gambling debt. That wasn't a problem anymore, though. Once he'd secured this land, he'd been able to sell his own, save the patch that held his home. He shuddered at the thought of what would have happened to him had he not paid on time.

"Nice bit of dirt you've got here," came a voice suddenly from behind him.

Startled, Drudder turned to find a tall, thin man with a smug grin on his unmistakably elfish face. In one hand was a piece of wood, in the other a knife. Intricate designs covered the wooden rod and, as he spoke, he casually traced out another symbol. Drudder knew the man all too well. He was the fellow in charge of placing the bets down at the races, the one who had kindly allowed him to gamble away more than a year's earnings on credit. After a string of losses, he was also the man in charge of collecting. The sight of the knife made him cringe.

"What are you doing here? You . . . you got the money, right?" Drudder stammered.

"Oh, yes, yes, my friend. I am here on other business. By the way, I heard about that fire. Terrible tragedy. But, then, it served you fairly well, didn't it?" remarked the visitor.

After a glance to see that no one else was in earshot, he smiled, "I'll say. Now all of this land is mine."

"Well . . . Not quite yours. Technically, it still belongs to the girl."

"Yeah, but the girl belongs to me."

"For now."

"What do you mean 'for now'? You told me that there wasn't any other family to worry about."

"Oh, there isn't, there isn't. But little girls grow up, and when she does, the land is hers."

" . . .I could . . . marry her to one of my sons."

"You could, you could." He nodded, carving another well-placed notch. "But then the land would be his, not yours."

" . . .So . . ." the man said slowly, brow furrowed in the unfamiliar activity of deep thought.

"Well, back before the unfortunate fire, you had realized, quite on your own, that if the owners of this land were to die, you would be able to claim it as your own, yes?"

" . . .Yes . . ." Drudder said slowly.

He remembered the conversation well. After a calm, frank explanation of the very severe consequences of not paying his debts, the strange man had remarked that he knew a fellow with family in this village. He'd just passed away and, thus, in the unlikely event that the whole Rinton household were to die, their land would be up for grabs, and Drudder himself would have a very strong claim to it. The hypothetical scenario had been laid out with remarkable detail. True, he never did specifically suggest that Drudder *do* anything, but he did everything but put the lit torch in his hand.

"And the survival of the girl is the only deviation from that sequence of events, yes?"

"Yes."

"Then it would seem that you could bring about the initially intended outcome by correcting that minor flaw."

"So . . ." he began, his mind slowly catching up to the logic, "you are saying I should kill the little girl, too."

"I am saying nothing of the sort. It would be despicable to even suggest it," he said, pausing to brush some shavings from the carving. "I am simply indicating that her death is the only way for this land to be irrevocably yours."

"All right . . . all right, plenty of dangerous jobs around. She's bound to have an accident."

"Considering the fact she survived a fire that killed the rest of her family, I am not certain simple misfortune can be trusted to do the job. And if you were considering helping fate along, you should know that more than a few suspicious eyes are turned in your direction already."

" . . .Well, what else is there?"

"Why, selflessness, my boy. You must put your village before yourself."

"I . . . I don't know what you mean . . ."

"Well, it just so happens I came to deliver a message to the church. It seems a note was received up north informing Conner Celeste about the Rinton tragedy. Conner, you'll recall, is the young man who I'd mentioned had died."

"Yeah . . ."

"Well, you never did ask me how he met his end, did you?"

"No . . ."

"Poison. Perhaps a poisoned knife, perhaps a poisoned claw or tooth. And not only that, but a dragon was seen near his body. Funny thing about dragons. They tend to carry a vendetta--"

"A what?"

"A grudge," he simplified with a roll of his eyes, "against whole families--"

"Can . . . dragons poison people?" Drudder asked, quickly falling behind in the conversation again.

"A venomous dragon is a rare but not unheard of occurrence. Please try to focus, I'm coming to a point. You see, if the dragon killed Connor, and it is seeking to exact some sort of vengeance on the whole of his family, then it would have come after the Rintons. It may have even started that fire," he led.

"No, but I--yeah, the *dragon* started that fire. Say, how did you know we had a dragon problem?"

"Word travels fast. Now, if the beast wants to punish the entire family, then it won't leave until it has the girl, yes?"

Drudder nodded slowly, struggling to connect the pieces, "So . . . You are saying I should--"

"No, Mr. Drudder. No. I am not saying you should do anything. I am merely musing out loud that were to you to offer the girl as a sacrifice to the dragon, it might appease the beast, simultaneously ending the drought, clearing you of any suspicion, securing the land for you once and for all, and making you a local hero. Any decision to do this contemptible thing would be yours alone!" the strange man growled.

"Okay, then . . ."

"Well, I'm off to deliver this message to the church. And good luck with your dragon problem."

Chapter 2

With that the strange man paced away, while Drudder hurried to the home of Delnick. That night, another meeting was called. By the time the relevant parties were gathered, Drudder was almost giddy with excitement. He had lit the fire that killed the Rintons, and the fact had haunted him from that day.

It would be nice to suggest that he felt guilty for what he'd done, but of the many things that troubled him, his conscience was not one. It wasn't that he was an evil man. Evil requires passion, ambition, motivation. Drudder didn't care enough to be evil. He didn't care about right, he didn't care about wrong. Right now, sacrificing the girl would solve every last problem he had. That was the only thing he cared about, and once he'd found something to care about, it was the only thing on his mind until it was done.

"Are you certain?" Delnick asked.

One does not become the man a village looks to for leadership by throwing children to monsters without good reason.

"Of course I'm certain! Listen, you heard what the priest said the note said. The man died from poison and there was a dragon. The dragon was the one that did it, it must have. Then the whole family dies in a fire. Dragons breathe fire. Now, when he couldn't kill the girl, he brings this drought down on all of us. This is the answer, Delnick. This is what we have to do. We have to . . . to . . . *appease* the beast," Drudder added, recalling the fancy-sounding word his mysterious adviser had used.

Delnick looked over the crowd. It was clear by the muttering and change in expressions that the thought of a quick and simple solution to their many problems appealed at least as much to them as it did to Drudder, with the added benefit that there would be no blood on *their* hands. On the surface, it is leaders who guide their people, but this is almost never true. A leader who takes his people where they don't want to go seldom remains a leader for long, so leadership instead becomes the art of assuring obedience by ordering to be done what would have been done in the first place. He didn't like it, but if the village felt that this was the only way, then he would see that it was so.

"Right. Kruck, when do these things come out to hunt?" Delnick asked.

"I had my run-in 'round about dusk," he replied.

"Then tomorrow, a bit before the sun sets, I want you to take the little girl to Teller's Pit and . . . leave her there. Don't tell her what she's in for. The least we can do is give her this last day without fear," Delnick decreed sadly.

With that, the frightened, unsure minds of the town left, set on the only desperate solution to present itself. Jade had her evening meal that night unaware that it would be her last, and woke the following morning to find that there would be no work that day. Instead, Drudder pulled her aside.

"You there . . . er, Jade. I want you to come with me. The boys will see to the field today," he explained to her.

"Why? Where are we going?" she asked.

"To Teller's Pit. We're going to . . . try to find a way to get some water," he said.

"And I get to come?" she said.

"Yeah, yeah. You get to come."

Jade grinned ear to ear. This was the first time her caretaker had taken any sort of interest in her, and the first time in ages that she'd had a break from the daily routine. She didn't need to know why.

"Thank you!" she said, throwing her arms around Drudder.

For just a moment the man felt a pang of conscience. For just a moment.

"What should I bring? What are we going to do?" she asked.

"It is just a little walk. You don't need to bring anything. Just you, me, and a few of the other fellows from around town. We'll take a nice walk, look around a bit, and then come back."

"Okay!" she said cheerfully.

Drudder, Jade, and three of the more able-bodied men of the town set off just as the sun was beginning to droop. The little girl's spirits were sky high. She was hungrier and thirstier than she'd been in weeks--but, for the first time since the loss of her parents, someone was treating her like she actually existed. The person she had been before the tragedy, long buried beneath impenetrable sadness, was beginning to show. After barely uttering a word for so long, she seemed to be making up for lost time. Questions were coming in a continuous stream, with little regard for the fact that there were no answers.

"Is Teller's Pit far? Have we ever looked there for water before? We should do this more often . . ." she babbled as they continued along.

Just over an hour and just under two hundred questions later, the group reached their destination. Teller's Pit was aptly named. Dry, brittle grass tapered off to a rocky lip that fell sharply off for a few dozen feet. At its bottom, a bed of gravel and debris took on a gentler slope as it led into a low-roofed tunnel. As the four men drew closer to it, they became visibly tense and nervous. Only the girl was oblivious to the danger that lurked within.

"W-o-o-ow," Jade said, inching up to its edge and peering in. "Are we going to explore it?"

"No. But I want you to stay here while the rest of us look around a bit. Don't move from this spot, no matter what, and keep a good eye on that cave. We'll be back in a while," Drudder said, eying the pit anxiously.

"Okay! I hope you find water," she said cheerfully, as the men who had brought her retreated at a near run.

For a few minutes, Jade paced about the edge of the pit, pleased that she'd been given something important to do. As the minutes turned to hours, and the sky began to redden, boredom set in. She kicked a few stones, took off her shoes to give her feet some air, and tried not to think about how thirsty she was. With a sigh, she gathered up an armful of stones and began to throw them, one by one, into the pit.

One of them took an odd bounce and tumbled into the tunnel, clacking and echoing as it went. At the sound of the echoes, the mouth of the tunnel became her new target, with each stone echoing louder and bouncing further. She was listening to the final stone click along in the darkness when something suddenly felt wrong. The clicking was getting louder, not quieter. She stared curiously at the mouth of the cave. As she did, memories she'd thrust aside for the last few weeks began to work their way to the surface again. Finally, a creature emerged from the mouth of the cave, and Jade realized that she was seeing it for the second time.

She caught only the merest glimpse of it, but in half that time it had burned itself into her memory. Emerald green scales armored its back, its belly protected by yellow plates. At the end of a cruel, serpentine neck was a vicious reptilian head, set with piecing, yellow-gold eyes. Jade was already sprinting away, screaming at the top of her lungs, by the time it fully emerged from the shadows. At the sound of wings unfurling, she turned to see the monster launch from the mouth of the pit and into the air. Jade doubled her speed as the shadow swept across the ground, and when the earth shook with the creature's landing, she doubled it again, moving with a speed only fear could allow.

At the midpoint between the pit and the town, Drudder waited. The others had wanted to return to the town, but he convinced them to remain. Maybe it was the fact that the fire had failed to kill her. Maybe it was the fact that he was only now realizing how tenuous his grip on the land that rightly belonged to her was. Whatever the reason, he wanted to be absolutely certain the job was done. And so he was dutifully watching the trail when the terrified girl, quite alive, came trudging through the trees. Upon seeing him, the girl found the strength to run to him for protection.

Rather than comfort her, Drudder took her firmly by the shoulders.

"Mr. Drudder, I was right, I did see a dragon! It was in the pit! It almost got me!" she sobbed.

"I know there was a dragon, how did you get away from it!?" he growled.

"I ran! Y-you knew there was a dragon?"

"Of course we knew there was a dragon! You can't just *run away* from a dragon. What did you do!?" raved one of the others, a man called Mirren.

"I swear! I swear I just ran! I don't understand what--"

"I'll tell you how she did it. She's a witch!" Drudder said in a tone more of realization than accusation, "She *must* be a witch. She survived that fire that killed her family. The only land that grows anything is the land *she* works. Now she escapes a dragon!? She's got to be a witch!"

"What? No! No, I--" she objected tearfully.

Drudder quickly threw a hand over her mouth.

"I won't have you speaking any spells, girl," he said, with the desperation of a man who believes he may have killed the family of a girl who could turn him onto a toad. "Tie her up, and gag her. Quick!"

Ropes and rags were produced, brought along in case the girl were to realize her fate and try to escape. Her hands were bound behind her back, her feet bound together, and a rag tied across her mouth.

"What do we do now?" asked Mirren, nearly manic with anxiety.

"We take her back and we feed her to the dragon," Drudder replied.

"What? No! She probably killed it with her magic!"

"We would have heard or seen it if someone killed something that size with magic."

"Well, then that monster is still out there! It will kill us!"

"Would you rather die of thirst from the drought?"

"Yes! It takes longer! Besides, maybe it isn't the dragon causing the drought. Maybe it's the witch."

"Then feeding the witch to the dragon will solve both problems, won't it?"

"You're on your own, Drudder. Me and . . .--hey, wait for me!" called Mirren after the others, who had already set off quickly back to town.

Drudder looked to the bound girl, then to the town, and finally toward Teller's Pit. With a grit of his teeth, he stooped, clutched the girl under an arm, and set off toward the pit. As he walked, he ranted.

"It is the dragon causing the drought. People will die if it doesn't rain. So we send you to appease the dragon, and you run? Do you *want* the drought to continue? Not me. No, this is the right thing to do. This is . . . this is for the greater good!" he muttered almost maniacally. "That's why I'm doing it. It has to be done."

It was the act of a man desperate to convince himself. His pace was brisk, practically a run, despite having to carry Jade. It had to be. He was feeding a little girl to a wild beast. It was a horrific act, even with the purest of intentions, and his were anything but pure. Drudder was in a race against his own conscience.

The edge of Teller's Pit came into view. He stepped up to the rocky lip, girl over his shoulder. He gathered what little will he had left and took her into his arms. All he had to do was throw her down, and all of his problems would be over. He would inherit the land once and for all. He would not be suspected. The drought would end. It was all so simple, clean cut. It would all be over. He extended his arms. All he had to do was to let go . . .

The ground shook, a shadow slipping over Drudder. He turned. There were legs, scales, and shadows. He looked up . . . and up . . . and up . . .

The dragon's head hung directly above his own. Quite without his permission, his arms lowered the girl. She fell to his feet.

"She . . . she's yours! Take her!" He shuddered.

The dragon, eyes locked and teeth bared, circled to the side. Drudder bolted, a panicked run taking him madly back toward the town. The beast unleashed a bloodcurdling roar and followed. The footsteps retreated into the distance and, for a moment, Jade was alone. She struggled desperately, but the ropes around her hands and feet were far too tight and far too strong. The best she could manage was to dislodge the gag from her mouth and wail for help. She screamed as loud as she could, and for as long as she could, until a sound between cries rendered her silent. The footsteps were returning.

Jade shut her eyes tight and tried to stay silent as the monster stalked closer, hoping perhaps it would not notice her. Despite the warmth of the sun, she could not stop trembling. The dragon's terrible claws clicked against the stone of the pit's edge. The monster did not run, it did not pounce. It almost seemed cautious in its approach, turning what Jade had feared would be a sudden painful end into a torturous wait. Finally, the dragon stopped. Though she did not dare open her eyes, the little girl could feel it towering over her.

For a moment, the only sounds were the vast, hissing breaths of the monster and her own terrified whimpers. Then came the rumble, a sound felt as much as heard. It was a growl, deep and grating, more like pounding hammers or distant war drums than a sound a creature could make. Steadily, it grew stronger, until it shook the ground and rattled Jade's bones.

There was a sudden, forceful nudge at her arm that flipped her onto her stomach. For an instant, she felt the dragon's steaming breath on the back of her neck. She braced herself for the end. The growl grew louder and sharper in tone as it opened its mouth. Then came a firm tug at the nape of her shirt and she was wrenched into the air.

The terrified girl could stifle her screams no longer. She cried and wailed harder and harder as the beast leaped into the pit and plodded along, its latest morsel dangling from its teeth. Breath from its nostrils hissed in her ears as she swung by her tattered shirt, traveling deeper and deeper into the cave. The journey was a long one, exhaustion and a scoured throat reducing her cries to quiet whimpers long before it reached its end. Time dulled the edge of her fear enough to let her mind wander. Where could it be bringing her? Her thoughts drifted to spring, to mother birds bringing worms to their nests. Nests filled with gaping, hungry mouths . . . She found the strength to scream again.

When even the renewed terror was not enough to convince her to torture her parched throat any longer, she hesitantly opened her eyes. It did no good. The light from the mouth of the cave was long gone. Blackness surrounded her. Still, the dragon walked onward. Its growl had subsided, leaving only the clicking of claw on stone and the huff of hot breath to remind her of that which carried her. In time her aged shirt began to tear. The beast lowered her in the darkness, wrapping her instead with its tail and lifting her to continue the terrible journey.

After what seemed like hours, Jade's red, tear-drenched eyes caught a glimpse of light on the walls around her as she was carried behind the beast. Were they heading back to the mouth of the cave? She twisted her neck and strained to see the approaching glow. It was certainly the sun, but it was not the craggy pit that she'd been carried into. As she was brought nearer, it was certain that the beast had hauled her to a second cave entrance.

The dragon loosened its tail and Jade dropped to the dry, sandy ground outside the cave. She tried to roll over, but the monster's snout nudged the small of her back, forcing her down. Before she could struggle any more, she felt a razor sharp tooth graze her wrist. This was it. The end. Now there was a scrape at her knuckles. Jade prayed that the beast would be swift. The bindings of her wrists pulled painfully tight . . . and then fell loose.

After a moment, the ropes that bound her feet were similarly sheared through. The young girl remained trembling on the ground for a moment. Steadily, the footsteps of the dragon retreated. She climbed to her feet, shaking. It had spared her. More than that, it had freed her.

In times of great danger, the body acts in its own defense long before the mind has had time to prepare orders. She had already run a dozen strides before she had realized she had even moved. When Jade was finally able to overrule her survival instincts, she slid to a stop and fought to catch her breath. Where was she going? She didn't know where she was, though that hardly mattered. She could probably find her way back to the city, but there was no use even trying. If she went back now, they would never believe that she wasn't a witch. No one should be able to survive being a bound offering. Even if they did let her return, Drudder had said that the dragon was causing the drought. If it didn't have her, the horrible thing wouldn't let the rains come and the town would wither away. For the good of her home, and against her every instinct, she began to walk back to the cave.

With each step, the fear smoldering in her stomach burned hotter. The sandy ground with its prickly, parched grass dwindled to rough, cold stone. The monster had dangled her for a long time. The cave must be enormous. How would she even find the beast? Ahead was a wall of blackness. It came sharply and suddenly, as though the light itself was afraid to delve any deeper. Perhaps with good reason. From the darkness came the thundering growl once more.

The dragon emerged from the pitch. It must have been lurking there, just out of sight, as if hiding behind a black curtain. The strength drained from Jade's legs. Slowly, she lowered herself to the ground and let her head sag. The growl grew stronger as the beast plodded the few remaining steps toward her. Its snout was inches from the top of her head. She trembled, but did not run. This was for the others. This was to end the drought. She repeated the words over and over again in her mind in a failing attempt to stem the urge to flee.

The terrible nostrils drew in a long, slow breath, releasing it all at once as a terrible roar. It was earsplitting, rebounding off of the walls in a chorus of echoes. The gale of scalding hot breath hit her with all of the fury of a raging storm. Her hair rushed back, tears poured down her face, but she held firm.

When she raised her eyes, the beast was barely visible as a gleam of eyes and a vague form beyond the edge of the darkness again. Jade locked the eyes in her gaze. The rumble began again, but it brought with it something more startling than anything that came before it. A voice.

"Leave," it spoke.

The word folded seamlessly with the growl, so much so that she for a moment doubted she had heard it at all.

"N-no," she managed, when she finally found her voice.

"Have you no sense?" the beast thundered.

Its voice was different this time. Not smooth, but smoother. There was a power and depth to it that almost made it more terrifying than the roar. It was a voice that sliced to the very core of the mind, deep and commanding.

"You h-have to e-eat me."

The gleaming eyes narrowed.

"No."

The growl rumbled behind the word, like a hammer driving a spike home. Jade shut her eyes tight, tears flowing anew. With a heroic effort, she managed to utter words that likely had never been spoken before.

"Please eat me?"

She offered the words up imploringly, pitifully. Nothing about this made sense anymore. She was a sacrifice. It was supposed to be terrifying. It was supposed to be deadly. It was *not* supposed to be difficult. She shouldn't have to convince the terrible beast to play its role. She was lost and unsure, her mind spinning. In a way, it was far worse than the fear, which had at least been certain.

"Why would you beg for death?" grumbled the dragon, the merest hint of frustration in its voice.

"They sent me to . . . to 'pease you," she said uncertainly.

After a few silent moments, the dragon replied.

"They sent you to appease me?" offered the beast.

Jade nodded vigorously and sniffled, grateful that she appeared to be making progress.

"Then go to your people and tell them that I am appeased," the dragon instructed.

The words took a moment to penetrate the layers of fear and confusion, but when they did, they came with a glimmer of hope that fairly gleamed from Jade's eyes.

"R-really?" she asked, heart leaping.

"Yes," the creature replied.

"So you'll stop the drought?"

The silence lasted longer this time. Slowly, the dragon slid from the darkness. Jade clung desperately to the thread of hope. For the first time, she was looking upon the creature with at least a tiny fraction of her wits about her. Its face, fearsome though it was, had another quality to it. Though it was subtle and difficult to identify, there was a glimmer of emotion in its features. It was in the twist of its mouth, the flare of its nostrils, and, more than anything else, in its eyes. There was weariness, frustration and, perhaps, a hint of . . . regret?

"No."

"But, but that's why I had to a-ppease you. They said that the drought wouldn't end until you were a-ppeased. You have to end it! People are starving! Animals are dying of thirst!" she urged desperately, her last slim chance slipping away.

"Go," the creature ordered, turning and slipping back into the shadows.

"I can't go back! They think I know magic, and if I come back now, they'll never believe I don't, and they'll kill me, and even if they don't, without water the crops won't grow and, and--"

The words came in a torrent. More followed, but they were nothing but a mangle of bawling sobs. Mind clouded by desperation and eyes clouded by tears, she charged into the darkness. She didn't know what she was hoping to achieve with the act. All she knew was that her life, which by rights should have ended by now, was hopelessly out of control, and somewhere in the darkness was a beast that had to answer for it.

Her bare feet pounded against the cool floor for a few steps until, without warning, the floor was no longer there to meet her. Jade tumbled forward onto what turned out to be a sudden, steep slope. She crashed and flailed painfully along the incline until it turned sharply to level ground once more. The young girl's head struck the floor with the full force of the fall.

Red and white sparks filled her vision. She slipped to the very edge of consciousness. There was pain, but it was far away. Though she could not see, she felt that the whole of the cave was spinning wildly. The world faded in and out around her, as though everything was happening on the other side of thick curtains. Was she moving? Was something echoing? She had neither the wits to know nor the will to find out.

Chapter 3

When the daze came to an end, it did so slowly. She became aware of a flickering yellow light and a faint crackling noise. A fire? The ground beneath her was not cold and hard. It wasn't ground at all. It felt almost like . . . cloth? When she tried to turn her head to see, the world seemed to whip around her so violently she held onto the mysterious bedding for fear of being thrown free.

When the bout of dizziness died down, she opened her eyes. What slowly came into focus was a pair of massive, amber-gold eyes. Now the emotion was clear, even to Jade's impaired mind. This creature was concerned.

The dragon was standing over her, not so much staring into her eyes as analyzing them.

"Speak," the beast demanded.

"Where am I?" Jade asked muzzily.

The dragon stalked quickly away, anger replacing the worry in its voice and features.

"What sort of a fool are you, charging into a dark cave. You could have been killed," grumbled the beast, as it set about a task beyond the range upon which Jade's eyes were currently willing to focus.

She eased herself up and tried to look about again, this time slowly. Her head felt two sizes too big, every motion threatening to topple her over. The dim light was coming from a weak fire in the corner of what looked to be a high-roofed chamber within the cave. From the darkness came the dragon, still muttering, with something clutched between its teeth.

"Where am I?" she asked again, trying to stand.

Almost immediately, she lost her balance. The dragon's tail snaked around her before she could hit the ground. It placed her back upon the pile of rags that had served as a bed.

"Sit!" the beast ordered through clenched teeth.

It lowered the bucket it was carrying before her.

"Drink."

Jade looked down. It was a large wooden bucket with a tin dipper. Her eyes widened. It was filled with water. She began to drink almost frantically. The precious liquid ran down her face and soaked her shirt as she desperately scooped it up. Her parched throat and cracked lips fairly sang with relief. The water had an inky and stagnant taste, but she didn't care. Jade drank until her stomach felt like it would burst, and when she couldn't swallow another drop she ladled the water over her head to feel the coolness trickle down her back.

When the bucket was empty, Jade paused for a moment. The combined effects of the blow to the head and the profound sense of relief from finally quenching her thirst was a potent one. For a time she simply sat, feeling the life return to her dehydrated body.

Gradually the facts of the current predicament began to trickle into her mind. Her vision had cleared enough to take in the sparse contents of the cavern. Here and there were scatterings of items. There didn't seem to be any rhyme or reason to them. Some piles seemed to be clothes and bags. Others were pots and pans. All seemed to be originally from chests, which were now splayed open and splintered. It made the cave look more like a field left behind by a traveling market than the home of a monster. Near the center was a handful of gold trinkets and coins mounded carefully. It was all very curious, and Jade's young and addled mind struggled to cope, but all she had learned thus far was that was little more demanding of one's attention than the presence of a dragon.

The beast was sitting beside the tiny pile of valuables, tail curled in front of it in a vaguely protective manner. Its eyes were locked on Jade. The stare was almost painfully intense, and unshakable. It made her feel small and helpless, like a cornered rabbit cowering from a wolf. Almost worse was the silence. Something as massive and deadly as a dragon ought to make a noise, even when standing still. Clearing a throat that was not dry for the first time in weeks, she spoke.

"Th-thank you for the water," she managed.

"You needed water," the dragon rumbled, as though somehow that was all that needed to be said.

"My people need water, too."

"Then they should get it."

"If . . . If you would bring back the rain . . ."

The cavern echoed with a deep growl.

"I'll do whatever you want me to. You said you were a-ppeased, but you aren't bringing back the rain, so you must not be."

The thumping growl continued to rumble.

"What would it take to a-ppease you?"

"Do you even know what that word means?"

"I . . . Uh . . . At first I thought it meant 'get eaten by' . . ."

"It means they want you to give me what I want so I won't be angry anymore."

"So . . . it *does* mean 'get eaten by'?"

"Why would I want to eat a little girl?"

"I don't know! You're a dragon! It's what dragons do! They come to towns and scare everybody, an' they capture maidens an' fight knights an', an' . . . an' cause droughts!" she raved, climbing to her feet again.

The voice of self-preservation within Jade gently suggested that screaming at a dragon was not a wise thing to do. Unfortunately, it was lost in the tangle of her mind. She was tired, she was hungry, her head was throbbing, and she was being asked questions she didn't know how to answer. The little girl was at the very end of her wits, and the dragon was the only one she could vent to, so it was going to get an earful.

"Why are you doing this? What did we ever do to you? It is bad enough that you take away the rain and keep it all for yourself," she cried, kicking the bucket away, "but then when we try to give you what you want, you won't take it! You roar and growl at me, then when I fall and get hurt, you bring me here and give me a drink!? Why? What is wrong with you!? What do you want!?"

"I want you to go back to your family and--"

"My family is dead!" she shrieked.

The sharp tone and sharper glare were enough to give even the dragon pause for a moment. Tears of anger and sadness trickled slowly down her cheeks.

"Your foster parents, then, and--"

"They aren't my foster parents. They only take care of me so they can use my family's land," she said coldly.

"You have no family?" the dragon asked.

"My brothers and sister and both of my parents died in a fire," said Jade, sniffling and attempting to stand tall, "so if you were sparing me to be nice, don't. There's no one left to cry when I'm gone."

"I am not going to kill you," the dragon rumbled, "and I cannot stop the drought."

"What do you mean you can't? You started it!"

"I have nothing to do with this drought."

"Don't lie--you have water and we don't! Where would you get water in a drought if you couldn't stop and start it whenever you want?"

"We are in a cave, deep underground. Dig deep enough and you often find water. Deepen your wells, or dig a new one."

"I . . . No! No, they wouldn't send me here to die if they weren't sure. They wouldn't sacrifice me unless they'd tried everything else!" Jade objected.

Even as the words left her mouth, she knew that they were false. The last of the water had only been gone for a few days before she had been thrown to the dragon. This hadn't been the last resort--it had been the first. Her eyes slowly lowered as the realization swept in.

"Your people were sure. It isn't the same as being correct."

She did not reply.

"Go back to them."

"I can't go back. They think I'm a witch, remember? There is no way that I could convince them you let me go. Unless . . . could you come with me? Could you tell them about letting me go, and about the drought and the wells?" she asked weakly.

"No."

"No . . . I guess it wouldn't have worked anyway. If they won't listen to me, why would they listen to you? And I don't want to go back, even if they would take me."

"You must."

"Why?"

"You need someone to take care of you."

"They threw me to you! They don't care about me. The only one who seems to care about me is . . . you."

The dragon seemed to stiffen at the words.

"Why? Why spare me? Why help me when I fell?"

"It doesn't matter. If you will not allow the people of this village to care for you, then we will find another."

"No!" she said, stomping her foot. "This is your fault! If you didn't show up, they wouldn't have blamed you, and then they wouldn't have tried to sacrifice me. Besides, they all knew me, and they were still willing to throw me in this cave. Strangers would be even worse. I've met a lot of people, and right now I don't like any of them. I've only met one dragon, and you've treated me much better than them."

"No," the beast growled.

"Why not? Why do you care?"

The silence fairly burned with the intensity of the beast's frustration.

"What is your name?"

"Jade."

"All of it."

"Jade Vera Rinton."

The dragon looked her in the eye and slowly approached her. When its snout was near enough to touch her head, the creature inhaled, long and deep. When it was through, it opened its eyes again. They gleamed with certainty. Wordlessly, her bizarre host returned to his meager hoard and sat again.

"You must be made safe."

"Why!?" the little girl cried impatiently.

"Because you are important. And because it is my purpose."

"I'm important?"

"Yes. Stay here. You need to eat," the dragon decided.

With that, the beast was gone. The speed at which the creature moved left Jade blinking. It was just a flurry of legs and wings, then nothing but the sound of retreating footsteps in the darkness.

Jade rubbed her stomach absentmindedly. She was hungry, though she wasn't sure how the dragon knew. Now alone, she had nothing to do but explore what little of the beast's den the light revealed. One of the bags had clearly been a merchant's wares. Inside were various bits of clothing, among them a pair of boots. They were nearly twice her size, but she put them on anyway, and tied them as best she could. Being in a dragon's den was bad enough, but being barefoot in a dragon's den seemed somehow worse. Once thus outfitted, she clomped over to the fire and tossed a few more shreds of broken chest onto it. Finally, she couldn't find anything to keep her from the room's center, where the tiny mound of gold sat.

It had not seemed like much beside the dragon, but the two heaping handfuls of coins and assorted gold trinkets was by far the most money she'd seen in one place. She was still marveling at it when the beast arrived, clutching an entire stag.

"Get away from there!" It barked.

Jade stumbled backward. The dragon nudged its kill toward her.

"Eat."

Jade looked at the still-cooling prey.

"I can't eat a whole deer."

"Then eat some of it."

"Could you cut it for me?"

The dragon looked to its prize, then to the girl. With a grunt of rising annoyance, it set to work butchering the deer. It was a fairly delicate task for a dragon's claws. Jade looked away quickly and tried to ignore the gruesome sounds of her host at work.

"Do . . . do you have a name?" she asked, eyes still averted.

"Halfax," rumbled the beast, in a slurred manner that implied its mouth was involved in its current task.

"Ha'fax." she said.

"Hal-fax," it repeated, stopping briefly to glare at the back of her head.

"Hal Fax," she tried again. When no correction came, she continued. "And Hal, you are a . . . boy, right? A boy dragon?"

"Yes," he said, the statement punctuated with a deliberate snap of bone.

"W-where did all of these chests come from?" she asked.

"I stole them."

"Did . . . did you kill people for them?"

"No. Here."

A piece of meat dropped onto the ground beside her, a good deal larger than she needed, and a good deal sloppier than a butcher would have provided. Another little girl might have been horrified by the sight, but Jade had grown up on a farm in very hard times. She knew how her meals were made.

"Eat," he ordered.

"I need it cooked."

"You don't *need* it cooked."

"Uh-huh. I'll get sick if I eat raw meat."

"You will?" the dragon asked, brow furrowed.

Jade nodded vigorously.

"I don't know how to do that."

"I can do it!" Jade said, running to one of the mounds where she'd seen pots and pan. "Mommy lets me . . . *Let* me help her sometimes."

She hauled a massive iron pot from the pile and dragged it over to the meat. Once the formidable piece of venison was inside, no amount of tugging would move the pot.

"Um, could you put this on the fire?" she asked.

The beast reached out and clutched the small cauldron. It was like a toy ball in his hand-like paw. He dropped it on the flames.

"Now we wait until the pot heats up, and then--"

She was interrupted when Halfax launched a tongue of flame at the pot. Instantly, the black iron was sizzling hot.

Jade swallowed hard.

"Now what?" he asked.

"We wait until it is done."

"How long?"

Jade shrugged, adding, "'Til it's done."

"And you need to do this every time you eat?"

"Yes."

Halfax made an increasingly familiar grumble of frustration.

"Hal. Why did you--"

"Halfax."

"You mean Fax isn't your family name?"

"I have no family name."

"Oh. Well, can I call you Hal? For short?"

"Very well."

"Why did you steal all of these chests, Hal?"

"For gold," the creature replied, curling his tail about the mound once more.

"Why do you want gold?"

"Because I must have it."

"Why?"

"Because I must."

"But why must you?"

"I simply must. I do not feel at ease unless I have some."

"Why not?"

"Why do you ask so many questions?"

"I'm curious."

"And why is that?"

Jade shrugged.

"It is for the same reason that I seek gold. It is what we are."

Jade seemed satisfied with this answer. The merciful silence did not last long.

"Do you think it will rain soon?" she asked.

"I do not know."

"Do you think the villagers will figure out about the wells? Or about the water in here?"

"They tried to solve the problem of a drought by feeding a little girl to a dragon. I very much doubt they will find the proper solution on their own."

"Do you think they'll starve or dry up before it rains?"

"I don't care."

"Well, I do. Just because they're mean and stupid doesn't mean I want them to die."

"You can go back to them," he began hopefully, "and tell--"

"No!" she interrupted. "Think of something else."

The dragon glared at Jade once again. She stared back, unflinching.

"Can anyone in your village read?"

"I think the preacher can."

"Can you write?"

Jade shook her head.

"Find something to write on."

A bit of digging eventually turned up a shingle of wood that bore a carving of an anvil on one side and nothing on the other. Evidently one of the stolen chests had belonged to a blacksmith. She scurried back to the dragon, who was scratching something into the cave floor.

"You know how to write?" she said, astonished.

"Yes."

He reached into the flames and pulled a sliver of charred wood.

"Here. Copy these shapes."

Jade carefully traced out the shapes as she saw them. Many times the beast had to correct her. While she was very good at scratching the correct letter on the plank with the charred wood, the importance of things like order and orientation eluded her. With some coaching, and quite a bit of wiping away mistakes, by the time the meat had finished cooking, she'd managed to render a mostly legible message.

When she was through, she had Halfax pull the meal from the fire. No amount of searching among the scattered goods in the cave turned up anything resembling dinnerware. Instead, the blacksmith's pile revealed a knife and a half-completed buckler, which, in a pinch, could serve as a plate. With some difficulty, she managed to hack off a piece of the inexpertly prepared meal that was small enough to chew. The roast managed to be nearly burnt on the outside and nearly raw on the inside. It was, however, edible, and there was a lot of it. For Jade, who hadn't eaten her fill in weeks, it was a banquet.

"What does it say?" she asked, gnawing at a charred chunk of venison.

"Dig deep for water or look in cave," he replied.

"That's it? All of that writing for that?" she said, eying the crude letter doubtfully. "Well, now what?"

"I will leave it in the town."

"But what if they come to the cave for water?"

"We will not be here. Tonight we leave."

"Why?"

"Because once I enter the town, things will become difficult for me. And because we need to find someplace with people willing to take care of you. For now, you sleep."

Jade ate her fill and curled up on the pile of rags, falling asleep with a full stomach for the first time in what seemed like an eternity. She slept soundly until she was awakened by an odd jingling sound. She opened her eyes to a curious sight. Halfax had his head hanging over the tiny pile of gold, his tongue deftly flicking the coins and trinkets into his mouth.

"Why are you eating your gold?" she asked with a giggle.

"I am carrying it in my mouth," he slurred.

"Wouldn't a bag be easier?"

"I would need to carry the bag in my mouth. Take what you need, but only what you can carry. We are leaving."

"Only what I can carry? Aren't you going to help?"

"No. I am a guardian, not a servant."

"Okay," Jade said sulkily.

She found a smaller pan, an oversized robe, and a pair of bags. Stuffing the buckler-turned-plate, the knife, and the pan into one bag, she walked up to Halfax. As he managed to flick the last coin into his mouth, she held the second bag open.

"Spit," she said.

"What?" he said, the sound garbled.

"Spit the gold in the bag. I'll carry it for you."

"Why?"

"Because you're my friend."

After a long, measuring stare, he opened his mouth. The coins and jewelry, along with a fair amount of drool, spilled into the bag.

"Ew." Jade grimaced.

Then she snatched up the cold remains of the roast and ate it, along with some more of the cave spring's water. As she did, she spotted a heavily-used oil lantern among the debris and lit it from the flames, singeing her fingers in the process. She cooled her hand in the bucket of water. A thought occurred to her.

"What are we going to do for water?" she asked.

"We will find it along the way."

"Okay," she said, dropping the dipper into her bag.

The small bag of gold and large bag of supplies strapped to her back, combined with the oversized clothes and the dangling lantern, made Jade look as though one of the mounds of random goods had decided to get up and walk away. Halfax padded slowly along the twisting passages of the cave, careful not to let the little girl fall behind. Even so, Jade had to hurry to keep up. The light of the lantern didn't cut far into the darkness of the cave, and the last thing that she wanted was to be left behind.

It was the dead of night when they left the cave. The dragon led the way to the nearest forest, and the pair walked just out of sight of the roadside away from Jade's town and toward the next. The trip took most of the night, but when they were as near to the place as Halfax dared to go, he turned to Jade.

"Go inside and find someone to take care of you," he ordered.

"But I've never been to this town. I don't even know what it is called," Jade objected.

"There are humans here. They will take care of you."

"But--"

"Go!" he growled.

Jade reluctantly trudged into town while Halfax waited and watched. Until the sun rose, the little girl simply sat in the city square and waited. As day came and the people began to go about their daily lives, the square became active. Few of the people spoke to Jade. Indeed, most seemed not to notice her. Those who did spoke only briefly. The day wore on with the most significant interaction being a kindly old woman who gave Jade a sweet bun. When the sun began to set, Jade trudged back to the forest.

"What happened?"

"Nothing! People didn't pay any attention to me!"

"Did you tell them you needed a home?"

"Uh-huh."

"Why didn't they help you?"

"People don't want another thing to worry about." Jade shrugged, then added, "I'm tired and hungry and thirsty."

Growling quietly, Halfax tracked down a meal and a source of water. Over the next few days, the process repeated itself. They would travel as far as they could, making their way from cover to cover in the night. When they reached a town, Jade would enter. Invariably, she returned to Halfax at night exhausted, hungry, and ignored. Some people were friendly. Some were even concerned, offering to help her find her lost family. When told that she had none and that she needed a home, most would do little more than offer encouragement and empathy.

When they reached a third city, a young man showed a sudden and dedicated interest in her, even taking her to a tavern for a meal. Halfax was hopeful that she had finally found a caregiver . . . until she came running back to him in tears at nightfall, the bag of gold taken. By the time she awoke in the morning, the bag was by her side again.

"How did you get the gold back?" she asked as she finished a meal.

"Never mind," Halfax grumbled. "This way. There is another village to the--"

"No!" she objected. "No, no, no, no!"

Halfax simply marched on.

"I'm not going any farther. No one is going to take a little girl by herself. We could go to any village you want. Maybe one of them will put me in an orphanage. And I *don't* wanna go in an orphanage."

"You are an orphan. You belong in an orphanage."

"I. Don't. Wanna," she said firmly.

"They will be able to care for you."

"And you can't? I'm not hungry and I'm not thirsty. That's better than my last home."

"You cannot live in a field or a cave."

"Why not?"

"Because you are a little girl."

"Then buy a house. You have gold. Plenty of it."

"I cannot live in a house, and I cannot be your caretaker."

"Why not?"

"Because I am a dragon."

"So what? Who made these rules? An' who says we need to follow them? Why do we have to do things just because you are what you are and I am what I am? You're a big scary dragon! You don't need to follow rules! And you've taken care of me better than anyone but my parents. You are my friend, Hal! I know you and I trust you. Why would you want me to be with strangers?"

"Because they--"

"No! I don't care! I'm going with you. You just pick a place and that's where we live. And if you try to leave me somewhere, I'll run away and find you, because I wanna stay with you and that's that," she declared, stomping her foot and crossing her arms.

Halfax clenched his claws deep into the ground, narrowed his eyes, and glared at the little girl. She returned his gaze without a flinch. The stare-down continued for some time before, finally, Halfax released a hissing sigh.

"There is a tower I passed on the way here. It looked like it had been empty for some time. We may be able to go there."

"Really!?" she squealed in delight.

"It will be a long journey."

"Don't care."

"You will be alone there."

"I'll have you."

"It is far to the north, very cold."

"North is this way, right?" she asked, hurrying off.

With a second, more defeated sigh, Halfax lumbered off behind her.

"It is my purpose to see that you are safe. This journey is dangerous. I need to know that you can make it by yourself. If something happens to me, I need to know that you can find your own way to someplace safe. So if you ever need me to carry you, even for a moment, I will carry you to the nearest city and you will not leave until you find someone. Do you understand?"

"I don't need your help. Let's go!"

Chapter 4

And so the pair began their journey. Jade was unfailingly cheerful and upbeat now that Halfax was no longer sending her away. When a town was near, they traveled at night. When far from society, they almost never stopped moving, pausing just once each day to hunt down and prepare a meal and sleep.

For the dragon, the journey was horribly slow. For Jade, it was brisk and tiring, but not once did she complain. She merely walked, a smile on her face, and happily provided a nearly unbroken flow of words, most of which washed over Halfax without acknowledgment or reply. Nights were spent in the shelter of thick trees.

After three days, dark clouds began to form and the drought came to a sudden end. The skies opened, dumping sheets of rain onto the thirsty ground.

At first, Jade was overjoyed, frolicking in the downpour. The novelty quickly wore thin, however, and had she not been in the company of the dragon, the night would have been a difficult one. But the wet wood was hardly a problem when the dragon could use his fiery breath to start the camp fire, and a single raised wing was as good as a tent to keep the rain from her head. When the rain let up, they continued on, but the heavy clouds made the night black as pitch. The little girl lit her lantern, but it was not long before its reservoir ran low. Jade tapped nervously at the lamp as the flame flickered out on the dry wick.

"We . . . uh . . . we need to stop in the next town," Jade said shakily.

"We are heading into the mountains. No more towns."

"Then we need to go back. We need oil for the lamp."

"There is a moon, there are stars. Plenty of light."

"They're behind clouds!"

"Plenty of light," he repeated firmly.

"Not for me. I can barely see anything."

"You don't need to see anything. I will lead the way. Just stay close."

"But what if there are things out there? Monsters!"

"I am a bigger monster than anything the darkness might hide."

Jade paused at an imagined sound in the bushes, then scurried to catch up to Halfax. She grabbed the tip of his tail and gripped it anxiously. He tensed at her touch and stopped walking.

"What are you doing?" he asked without looking.

"I'm holding your tail," she said, squeezing it tighter as something scampered across the ground nearby.

"Why?"

"'Cause I don't want to lose you in the dark . . . An' it makes me feel better."

"Very well," he said finally.

For the rest of that night's travel, Jade continued to hold the dragon's tail as one might hold the hand of a big brother. Halfax had to walk in an awkward, deliberate gait to keep from waving his tail about and tugging it from her grip, but the little girl didn't seem to notice. She merely continued on, gratefully clutching the tail and keeping her eye on the darkness.

Within another day, the two had made it well into the mountains. The travel had been slow before, but now it was getting slower by the hour. Even on level ground, it took ten of the girl's strides to match one of the dragon's. Now that the mountainside was getting steeper, the beast was often left waiting for minutes while Jade struggled to pull herself up the rocky slope. When she reached the first level patch in what seemed like ages, the girl sat on the ground and fought to catch her breath.

"I just . . . I need to . . . I can't . . . catch my breath," she wheezed.

The dragon watched her as she slowly recovered. When her breathing was almost normal, she struggled to her feet, ready to move on. The young girl raised her eyes to find Halfax crouching and leaning his shoulder low.

"What are you--"

"Get on my back," he ordered.

"No!" she objected, trying to shove him angrily. She only succeeded in pushing herself back. "I told you I can do it by myself!"

"I am not going to take you back to a town."

"You said you would . . ."

"I am saying different now."

"You promise? You promise not to take me back?"

"Yes."

"Say it. Say 'I promise to take care of you forever.'"

Halfax stood and turned, placing his face inches from her own.

"I promise to take care of you . . . forever," he said.

Jade stepped forward and wrapped the dragon's neck in a tight hug.

"Thank you," she whispered.

The dragon shuddered uneasily at the gesture of affection.

"Yes . . . you are . . . we should hurry. We've wasted enough time," he stuttered when the embrace lingered.

Climbing atop the beast proved awkward. It took a boost from Halfax's tail before she finally managed to take a seat at the base of his neck. As smoothly as he could, the dragon rose. Jade's frantic grip on his neck suggested it hadn't been quite smooth enough.

"Easy. Go slow," she urged.

Even at the barely walking pace that Halfax maintained at Jade's behest, the journey became a much swifter one. Icy patches were no match for the dragon's claws, and steep slopes meant little. Before long, the initial jolt of fear had worn off and Jade began to enjoy herself.

"You can go a little faster, if you want," she said.

His pace quickened to a trot. The gray mountainside slipping effortlessly below them, the steady rhythm of the trot, the breeze in her hair, they all combined into something Jade hadn't expected. It was . . . fun.

"Faster," she said tentatively.

Halfax quickened his pace to a slow run. The landscape was rushing by now. Gullies that Jade would have had to find a way around passed below them with one powerful leap. She had never traveled this fast in her life. Her little hands held tight to the scales of his back in fear of being thrown free. It was terrifying. At the same time, though, it was thrilling. She was charging across the mountaintops on the back of a wild dragon!

"Faster, faster, faster!" she squealed.

Soon the beast was sprinting. Great, bounding strides covered in seconds what had previously taken minutes. Jade gasped with exhilaration, and by the time Halfax slowed, half of a mountain was behind them and her heart was racing as fast as his.

#

By the end of the following day, they had reached their goal. Jade's eyes widened as their destination revealed itself. It was certainly a breathtaking sight. The building--and, indeed, the whole of the clearing that it occupied-- seemed to be experiencing entirely the wrong season. In the center of an icy gray forest, there was a bed of emerald green grass and a tree that bore juicy ripe apples. Along one edge, a stream flowed out from under a shell of ice, threaded a curving path through the clearing, and slipped back into the snow.

Though the setting was astounding, to the average adult the building itself wouldn't seem like anything special. It was little more than a humble wood cottage wrapped around the base of a precarious stone tower perhaps three stories tall. A large wooden shack extended from one side to form what had been formerly used as a stable, and the front door was splintered and broken. Nothing remarkable.

Jade, though, had grown up in a small farming village. She'd only seen a building half as tall a handful of times, so even the dilapidated stone spire was an object of wonder for her. Neither the spring clearing nor the stone tower was the first thing on her mind, however. No, to her the most important thing was . . .

"A wizard really lived here?" she piped, scrambling from the dragon's back and running up to it.

"Several, over the centuries."

"Who defeated them?" she asked.

"Defeated them?"

"Yeah! It must have been a great hero. Maybe Desmeres!"

She spoke of Desmeres Lumineblade, by far the most popular and enduring folk hero of the north. His story was one of two histories of a very turbulent time, and had become the generally accepted one. This was largely due to the fact that literacy and academics had fallen out of favor, and his was considerably shorter and easier to remember. The fact that it seldom bore any more than a passing resemblance to the truth was largely beside the point.

"Why would Desmeres have had to defeat them?" Halfax asked, surveying the structure for any dangers.

"Because he was a hero, and that's what heroes do! They kill wizards and dr--and other things," she said. "Look, an apple tree!"

Jade threw down her bags and scurried to the edge of the clearing where the tree stood, its branches heavy with fruit. After a few failed attempts at climbing, Jade looked imploringly to Halfax. He butted the lowest branch and down tumbled a handful of the apples. She eagerly scooped them up and bit juicily into one.

"It's a Myranda," she said sloppily. "My dad used to grow these."

She turned to toss the dragon one, but Halfax was busy investigating the tower.

"What are you doing?" she asked.

"Wizards protect their towers."

"With magic?"

"Yes."

"Can you find it just by searching?"

"You cannot find it without searching."

After scrutinizing every inch of the structure he could reach, all while the little girl noisily worked her way through two more apples, Halfax could find no sign of danger. He turned to Jade, but his mouth hadn't yet opened to give permission by the time she had dashed inside.

"Be careful!" Halfax urged.

"There's all sorts of stuff in here. Tables, chairs! Oh, look, a big fireplace. Everything is dusty though." She coughed.

Her voice and footsteps darted this way and that inside of her new home as she excitedly cataloged the contents. Soon she was spiraling up the stairs, peering out through missing bricks, until she reached the single room at the top.

"There is a great big bed up here! Here, shake this out!" she called, hurling a set of bedding out the window.

The dust-covered blankets managed to land squarely on the dragon's face. By the time he shook them free, Jade was outside again. She snatched up the bag of gold and hurried to the doors of the tiny stable.

"Come on!" she piped, tugging them open.

Halfax plodded over and peered inside.

"Look! You can sleep here! It is big enough, and there is a door right there that leads into the house and everything. I'll get it set up for you!" Jade trilled.

She dumped the meager handful of gold onto the ground in the center of the stable and crouched to carefully arrange it.

Halfax looked over the decrepit structure. It was completely bare; not even a scrap of rotten hay littered the floor. Whatever innate fear the looters may have had of a wizard's tower clearly did not protect this place. He turned back to the little girl. Jade looked up, the pile of gold at her feet now neatly stacked, and smiled expectantly at Halfax. He heaved a sigh.

In a series of slow, awkward maneuvers that took the better part of five minutes, the creature managed to squeeze into the stable. He filled it to capacity, so much so that he wasn't so much laying in it as he was wearing it. When he finally finished situating himself, he managed to twist his head to face the little girl. She was standing in the doorway, a smile lighting up her face.

"See? Perfect!"

#

Over the course of the next few days, Jade set about preparing the tower. With Halfax's help, she washed her bedding, cleaned up clutter, set out pots and pans. Slowly, the abandoned place began to change. There was life in it now. It was by no means a mansion; in fact, it was little more than a pair of large rooms around the base of the tower.

One room was an all-purpose sort, playing the role of entryway, dining room, workshop, and clearly anything else the former resident had in mind. It had a fireplace at one side, a long table with two chairs, and very little else. It was the sort of room one might imagine would be assembled by a man who lived alone and preferred it that way, built simply and sparingly.

One door led to the outside, another to the stable, a third to the kitchen. A closet with no apparent knob stood on one wall, and opposite was a stone arch that led to the tower. A staircase that seemed to be perpetually on the brink of collapse spiraled up to a room that looked to have been emptied in a hurry. There was a bed, another table, and a ring of dusty, vacant shelves covering every wall. Boxes, chests, and cabinets were everywhere, and all completely bare. It almost would have looked ransacked, save for the fact that looters were never so gentle.

At the moment, the little girl stood in the kitchen. Her eyes took in a simple sight, just a stove with food cooking atop it. She marveled as though it were a celestial event. There was a roof over her head again, food in the cupboard, a bed to sleep in. She'd had all of that when she was with the Drudders, but here there was something else.

Jade walked into the fresh spring air and peered into the wintery forest that surrounded her. Halfax was among the trees, eyes ever vigilant. He turned to her briefly, and she smiled. Here she had something she'd lacked with the

Drudders. Here she had someone who cared about her. That made this place something she hadn't had since the fire took her family. That made this place her home.

#

Jade had taken to sleeping in the tower. It was the only place that had a bed and she had no way to move it. It was a nice enough place to sleep, though. Three windows, the only parts of the wall not covered with empty shelves, let in plenty of light and fresh air. Thanks to the perpetual spring weather, she seldom needed more than a single blanket. There was only one real problem. A lifetime of waking in a room filled with family--be it her own sisters or her foster brothers--made nights without the sounds of others feel horribly empty. Sleep came slowly, and when it did come, all too often it brought terrible things. Things she wished with all of her heart she could forget.

Her eyes shot open from just such a dream, the images still stinging her mind. Try as she might, she could not shake them away, and she dare not try to sleep again with them in her head. If she did, she might return to the same terrible, terrible dream. Finally she pulled herself from bed, grabbed the blanket, and trudged to the stairs.

"Hal?" came Jade's voice meekly.

The dragon's eyes slid open, locked onto her. As far as Jade could tell, Halfax never slept at all. The faintest noise drew his instant and dedicated attention. Now his eyes fell upon the little girl, standing in the doorway of his cramped quarters and dragging her blanket.

"Tell me what is wrong," he commanded. When there was even the slightest hint of trouble, the beast did not ask questions, he demanded information.

"I had a bad dream," she whimpered.

"Oh. Good," he said, eyes closing once more.

"It's not good!" she objected, hurt.

"It is good, because dreams cannot hurt you. Go to sleep."

"Can I sleep in here with you?" she asked, a tremor in her voice.

"Why?"

"It would make me feel better."

"But why? There is nothing to be afraid of. It wasn't real."

"You know . . . you know how there are some things you don't understand about me . . . because I don't understand them about me?"

"Yes."

"This is one of those things."

"There isn't any room here," he objected.

Jade quietly climbed into the stable, crawling onto Halfax and nestling herself between his folded claws and the curve of his neck. The dragon held perfectly still. He wanted to object, to send her away. This wasn't the role he was meant to play. But . . . the very moment she rested her head upon him, he

33

could feel the fear in her drop away. He knew fear. He could smell it, hear it in the beat of a heart. Predators were sensitive to it, trained to detect it, to seek it out. She'd been terrified, but now the anxiety was nearly gone.

For a time, it seemed that she would sleep, but before long she began to stir. She tossed and turned, fidgeting under her blanket.

"I can't sleep," she mumbled.

"Try."

"I am, but I can't. Tell me a story," she said.

"I don't know any stories."

"You must know stories. What did your mother tell you when you couldn't sleep?"

"I never had trouble sleeping."

"Well, you must know some stories. You're a dragon. You're old. And knights fight you and things," She yawned.

Halfax heaved a long sigh that drifted into a faint, frustrated growl.

"Whoa . . ." Jade said, her voice thumping with the rumbling sound. "Your whole body shakes when you do that. Why are you doing that? Are you--"

"Just go to sleep," he grumbled sharply.

After a startled silence, "Okay," was the meek reply.

Again a few silent, still moments passed, and Halfax desperately hoped she'd drifted off. Then came a sniffle and the soft sound of gentle weeping.

"Are you crying?" he groaned.

"No," she managed between whimpers.

"Yes you are."

"Yeah."

"I didn't yell at you. That wasn't yelling," he defended.

"Yeah, it was . . . But that's not why I'm crying."

"Then why?"

"I miss my family," she sobbed.

"I told you that you were better off in the city with--"

"Not them!" she shouted angrily. "My real family. When I had a bad dream, Daddy would hold me and Mommy would tell me a story and I knew everything would be fine . . . But--but everything wasn't fine! They died . . . and . . . I'll never see them again. Why did I live and they die?"

She buried her face in the blanket against the dragon's neck and cried. Halfax could do nothing but listen. He simply did not know what he was supposed to do. This tiny thing, curled up against him, was so fragile. Such a fragile body, certainly, but diligence and care was all that was needed to protect a body. Her emotions were just as fragile, and he had nothing for them. It simply had never been expected of him, and he'd never imagined it would be. He felt helpless, lost. Finally, a thought crept to his mind.

"Do you want to know why you lived?"

"You know?"

With effort, Halfax managed to fetch a coin from his hoard.

"Flip this with your left hand and tell me how it lands."

She took the coin and flipped it in the air.

"It landed face-up."

"Flip it again, and again. As many times as you like. It always will."

Sure enough, half a dozen tries ended with the coin facing her each time.

"How did you know it would do that?"

"Because you are lucky. Because fate has great things in store for you."

"Lucky? But . . . but my family died. I was thrown out of my town!"

"You survived the fire, and you were thrown to the one creature dedicated to your protection. Your bloodline runs thick with luck. Sometimes impossibly bad. In your case, impossibly good. The flip of the coin is one of the signs. Heads for good luck, tails for bad."

"How do you know?"

"My mother. She did tell me one story," he said.

"She did?" Jade sniffed.

"Yes. But it is a very long story . . ."

"That's okay. You can finish it tomorrow, or the day after."

"And it happened a very long time ago."

"Then it really happened?" she asked, fascination pushing fear and sadness aside for a moment. "Tell me!"

Jade sniffed and cuddled closer, wrapping the blanket tightly around her.

"Many years ago before you, or I, or even my mother was born, there was a woman. Her name was Myranda . . ."

#

The tale was indeed a long one. It was a story of heroes and heroism, of a great war and the trying times that followed, a story familiar to Jade and yet so new. There were familiar names, like Desmeres, but the roles were different. Names she knew as great men were sinister or unscrupulous. Creatures she thought were monsters were selfless defenders.

Halfax was not a storyteller, and it showed. He spoke of his mother, Myn, and the adventures of she and her friends. He called them "the Chosen," and spoke of deeds great and small, but he told it as a spy might deliver a briefing. Simple, efficient accounts of events. There was little flavor or life to the words, but that made little difference to Jade. She stopped him often, urging him for details and descriptions, and painted the scenes in her mind.

When she slept, the events sprang to life, easily forcing aside the bleak dreams of old.

He continued the tale for weeks, reciting it every night until she fell asleep. When it was through, she urged him to begin again. And so he did--and as he did, the story evolved. He remembered her pleas for detail, and with each telling he included all she had asked for during the last. The tale would swell with each pass until it was dripping with detail and teeming with adventure. And even so, each time it ended, there came the same request.

"Tell me more!" Jade piped.

"There is no more to tell," Halfax grumbled.

"Sure there is. You said that your mother was Myn, the red dragon from the story, right?"

"Yes."

"Well, what happened to her after?"

Halfax sighed.

"She found a mate."

"Your dad?"

"Yes."

"What was he like?"

"He was a green dragon."

"Was he brave and smart like Myn?"

"He was strong. And loyal."

"Did you have any brothers and sisters?"

"Yes."

"What were their names? What happened to them?"

"Like me, they were given a line of Chosen to protect. Windsor was my brother, and he watched over the Lumineblade line, the line of Desmeres. Thorn was another brother, and he watched over the Chosen named Ether. Roka was my sister, she watched over the Chosen named Ivy. I was the youngest, and I watched over Myranda's line. Your line."

"Where are they now?"

"Gone."

"All of them? How?"

"The world changed. Dragons slipped from their brief place of respect and grew again to be feared. Men destroy those things they fear."

"That's so sad."

"It is the way of things."

"It shouldn't be."

She thought for a moment.

"You've been following my family for a very long time?"

"I have."

"What happened to them? To the ones before me?"

"Most that I guarded lived long lives. I could only protect one small branch, the strongest I could find, but in the years that I stood guard, only one died by the hand of another before he could continue the line. His death severed the line, and sent me looking for you."

"Who was he?"

"He was a man named Conner Celeste. Someone killed him with a poisoned dagger. I do not know why, but by the time I arrived, he was too far gone."

"Connor . . . I don't know the name. Tell me more. More about my family . . ."

Chapter 5

In time, the story did its job, chasing away the dark thoughts in the young girl's mind, filling in pieces of her family and past. No longer plagued by nightmares, Jade did everything she could to fill her time. Every now and then she would venture off into the woods, but such expeditions seldom lasted long. The woods were dangerous, a fact that Halfax never missed a chance to repeat, and when she wandered too far, the dragon would simply snatch her up with his teeth or his tail and deposit her back in the cottage. It became something of a game to see how long she could evade him, but Halfax soon became far too good at it for her to get very far. Instead, she found things to do around the cottage. A garden was planted and tended, furniture was arranged and rearranged. Every inch of the cottage was searched and explored.

It was during just such an exploration one day that something very curious happened. She was leaning on a stone below one of the windows in the tower when it suddenly slid out of place. She scrambled backward, afraid she would fall through the hole left behind. When she looked where the stone had been, though, rather than daylight and open air, there was a dark chamber with a mound of dusty sacks. Jade stuck her head out the window and looked on the other side of the wall. The stone she had pushed aside was still in place from the outside. There was no sign of, and certainly no room for, the massive crawlspace she had seen. Yet, sure enough, when she looked through the hole, there it was, a veritable warehouse mounded with bags. Quickly, she pulled one of the sacks from the impossible room and looked inside . . .

"Hal!"

Barely a heartbeat after the call came, Halfax came sliding out of the frozen forest and into the summery clearing.

"What!? What's wrong?" the beast demanded, scanning the glade for threats.

Jade appeared at the door of the cottage, struggling with a heavy sack.

"Nothing's wrong, silly. But look what I found!" she said, brimming with excitement.

The bag was filled with books of all sizes.

"There's lots more, too. There was a false wall in the tower that led to a whole big room full."

Halfax eyed the tower, then the little girl.

"It's magic!"

She dropped the bag and lifted a heavy tome from inside, pulling open the cover and flipping to a random page.

"What's this say?" she asked, eagerly jabbing the page with a finger.

Halfax peered down at the faded writings, brow furrowed as he hoisted the seldom-used skill of reading from the depths of his memory.

"The . . . primary methods and means of . . . expediting poison . . . expulsion and--"

"What does that mean? Ex-ped-iting."

"It means speeding up."

"Why didn't it say speeding up?"

"Because a wizard will never use a small word when a larger one is available."

"Wow. Read more!"

"No. This is a spell book. It is dangerous to read from one if you don't know magic."

"Oh. Well, what about this one?" she asked holding up a thin green book.

"That is a spell book, too."

"Well, help me find one that isn't," she instructed, pulling out the books one by one and laying them in the grass, "There's a bunch more if we can't find one here."

With a slight growl of irritation that Jade had long ago learned to ignore, he looked over the covers, twisting his head to read the several that were upside down. Finally, he reached out and tapped a cover with a claw.

"This. This is about wildlife."

"Read it, read it!" she squealed, bouncing up and down.

"No."

"*Please?*" she begged, drawing out the word to make it several syllables long.

"I will show you how to read, and you can read it yourself."

Jade's eyes could not have opened any wider. A look of incomparable joy saturated her every feature.

"Really?" she trilled.

"Yes. Put the books away for now and come back here."

Jade hastily gathered up the books and sprinted off. As she did, Halfax began to methodically etch the alphabet into the gravel of the cottage's pathway. This was a trait shared almost exclusively by the extraordinarily long-lived. Halfax tended to work toward the very long term. Teaching the girl would take time, but it would only have to be done once. More importantly, knowing how to read would help her when she finally chose to rejoin her own kind. And so he would teach her, just as he would teach her how to hunt. Just as he would teach her how to track. He would teach her every language he knew, every skill that could aid a human, and with each new skill and each new year she would need him less.

And then she would be off again, on her own, and he would be in the shadows. As he should be.

Halfax paused. He'd thought of that moment many times. The day she would leave. It was never far from his mind, his constant goal. This time, though, there was a glimmer of something else. For just a moment, his heart sank.

"Ready!" Jade chirped, shaking Halfax from his thoughts.

Halfax pointed to the first letter with a claw.

"This is Ay. It goes ay . . ."

Steadily the dragon guided her through the alphabet. Jade was a ravenous learner, and seemed able to remember each letter perfectly after only a few repetitions.

"That is Bee, it goes buh," Jade said, when Halfax pointed randomly to a letter some time later.

"Yes, now. What is this?" he asked, tracing a shape out on the ground.

"Jay, it goes juh."

He traced a second, and a third, and a fourth.

"Ay, it goes ay. Dee, it goes dee. Eee, it goes eee," she recited.

"Just the sounds now."

"Juh, ay, duh, eee." she said.

"Pretend the eee doesn't make a sound."

"Juh, ay, duh."

"Faster, fast as you can. Over and over."

"Juhayduh, jayduh, jayduh . . . *Jade!* Is . . . Is that how you spell my name!?"

Halfax nodded.

"I can read my name!" she said, leaping up and down, "Why doesn't the E make a sound in my name?"

"Because you have a strange language, and it does strange things. Most are far stranger."

"So it is like a code, almost?"

"I suppose."

Jade squealed with delight, clapping. "Keep going! I want to know it all!"

\#

The days and weeks that followed were filled to the brim with as much instruction as Halfax was willing to provide. Though Jade was willing and eager to learn, progress was slow. They had very few books that were written with a new reader in mind. Nonetheless, she kept at it, all the while glowing with pride, as though she were being let into a very small and very exclusive club.

In truth, she was. Books were anything but plentiful these days, and those who could read them were thoroughly distrusted. Too much knowledge, it was believed, could have terrible consequences. A long war and the terrible foes who fought it were the result of magic, and by extension knowledge. Thus, steps were taken by society as a whole to see to it that such a thing was not allowed to occur again. If that meant burning books and exiling those who knew how to use them--or, worse, knew how to create them--then so be it. It might not always have been the case--but it had been this way for as long as anyone could remember. These books were almost certainly hidden so well specifically to spare them the same fate.

The veritable library hidden within the wizard's tower was, not surprisingly, mostly on the subject of magic. There were still dozens and dozens of books on a wide variety of other subjects, however, and slowly but surely she began to piece her way through them. Days turned into weeks, weeks into months.

Jade learned much, and her interests grew well beyond the resources the tower and its clearing could provide. Reluctantly, Halfax agreed to take her to the edge of Ravenwood nearest to a city, a place called Rook, so that she could buy supplies and feed her curiosity. As she had no money of her own, and no way to earn any, these trips were financed entirely from the dragon's meager hoard.

The pair arrived back at the tower after just such a trip, and Jade leaped from his back.

"Here you go, Hal," Jade said, dropping a single gold coin onto the top of his hoard.

The dragon looked at the coin upon the greatly diminished pile of gold. A glimmer of disappointment showed on his usually impassive features. This most recent trip had seen three gold coins leave with Jade in exchange for replacements for the clothes she was rapidly growing out of, some tools, and the odd necessities like rope and flour. Only one coin had returned. Jade felt a pang of guilt. It was her fault that the gold was being spent, after all. And it was very important to him that he have it. There must be something she could do to make him feel better.

She looked to the gold, then the bag of tools. An idea dawned.

"Wait, I need that back," she said, snatching up the coin.

She scurried to the doorway and into the cottage. A chorus of clanks, with the occasional yelp of pain, began to ring out. After a few minutes, she scampered back, something conspicuously held behind her back.

"Bend down."

"Why?"

"Just bend down, I have something for you."

The dragon complied. A loop of rope was thrown over his head. He snatched the end of it and twisted his neck to see what she'd hung there.

It was the large gold coin, pounded a bit thinner and larger. A hole had been punched near one edge and a bit of rope threaded through. On the face was a collection of marks roughly pounded into the surface that spelled out HAL.

"Now you've got one piece of your hoard that will always be with you."

"One piece of gold is no hoard."

"Well . . . Well, maybe not, but look at the back of it!" Jade defended.

Halfax flipped the piece to find, crudely rendered, the word JADE.

"That way you know you've always got me. And I'm better than a pile of gold, right?"

Halfax looked the smiling little girl in the eyes. Dragons all had an almost inexplicably accurate sense of value. It helped them to build their hoards. It motivated them to protect their hoards. Most had an affinity to gold, but they were quite able to root out precious stones and other precious metals. There were even, Halfax knew, those able to appreciate the value of human things like art.

The one blind spot was sentiment. Only the most enlightened of his kind understood the incomparable value even the most common objects could take on when associated with the proper memories. But in that moment, Halfax understood. No human had ever given him a gift. That made this crude amulet--and this little girl--one of a kind. Treasures of the very rarest sort. And they both belonged to him.

"Thank you," he uttered.

#

More time passed. As Jade grew, so too did her knowledge and her skills. Her garden flourished, as having a dragon to help do things like till the ground made the speed and ease of maintaining it remarkable. She learned to mend her own clothes, and even tailor them. Books taught her to repair and improve the cottage, another task made immeasurably easier with the help of a dragon. The beast could push in nails the way a smaller being might push in tacks. She learned ways to preserve her food, make her own medicine, and use the tools she did have to craft tools she did not.

When she exhausted the books written in her own language, Halfax taught her the other languages he knew, and she read on. As the months turned to years, the journeys to the city became less frequent, less necessary. Life fell into a pleasant, predictable routine. It was a sort of life Halfax was not very used to, but one that was very, very welcome.

#

Such a comfortable life, and being a dragon with the wisdom and duty of Halfax, made Halfax sensitive to even the smallest changes. After several years of uneventful bliss, something felt wrong one day. Hunting had been difficult. The forest was a good hunting ground, and Jade never ate much, but the animals had been more alert this time. Something had them frightened even before he'd arrived. It was difficult to place, but whatever it was that had spooked them, he felt it, too. Something was near. Its presence hung like a fog in his mind.

As he dropped the day's kill, Halfax focused upon a specific point among the trees at the edge of the clearing. There was nothing there . . . and yet . . .

He took a step toward it . . .

"Hal, thank goodness! You took a long time, I thought something had happened to you," Jade said from the doorway.

She was almost fifteen years old now. She'd worked her way through most of the books, and each new thing she learned, she tried. The recent book on farming had led her to expand her little garden, and she was very proud of her efforts.

"Come around the back, I want to show you how good the strawberries are coming in."

The dragon cast a final glance into the trees before following.

At the edge of the clearing, like a wisp of smoke caught in the breeze, a patch of forest seemed to sweep away, leaving a tall, lean figure where before had been nothing. It was an elf, and by virtue of his race, based on his appearance, he could have been age twenty or two hundred. He held in his hand what may once have been a walking stick. Now it was covered so utterly with intricate emblems and sigils that it seemed too delicate to support its own weight, let alone his. His face bore the vague look of irritation.

"I do hate the lucky ones," he muttered with a slow shake of his head.

With that he turned and, with the same flourish as he appeared, vanished.

#

Far to the south, many days later, an aging woman looked to the door of her apothecary shop. It had been a busy day, and there would be no one else at this hour. She poured the contents of the mortar she'd been grinding at into a small glass jar. Carefully, the container was placed beside the dozens of identical ones that lined the shelves behind her.

The air was thick with the scent of dried herbs and boiling potions, and every available surface was cluttered with scales, burners, glassware, and other tools of the trade. She made her way to the heavy door, pushed it shut, and drew the bolt.

"Quite a business you have here," came a voice from behind her.

The woman turned to find the same tall, intellectual-looking elf from the forest inspecting one of the vials from the table. In his hand was the excessively carved walking staff.

"How did you get in here!?" the owner cried, brandishing a heavy glass bottle from the nearest counter.

"I don't intend to be answering many of your questions, so for your sake, I shall ignore that one. A far more pressing one shall present itself shortly."

"Get out of my--"

"A useful service you provide the people of this town. A treatment for cutleaf poisoning. A tricky thing to treat."

"I . . . I do what I can," she said nervously.

"No, no, you don't. You do what you want to. The treatment is tricky. The cure much less so. It was difficult to find, but once you know what it is, it is simply a matter of taking enough of the right ingredients. In order to merely treat the poisoning, you would have to measure far more precisely."

"H-how do you know that?"

"That is the question you ought to be asking, Damona. How do I know what I know? First let me tell you what else I know, then I'll tell you how. I would put the bottle down, if I were you. You are perilously close to making me feel unwelcome."

Shakily, she lowered the improvised weapon.

"Your name is Damona Tienne, no middle name. The fact that you have been able to concoct both a functional cure and modify it into merely a treatment shows that you have a firm understanding of magic. The fact that you call yourself an apothecary rather than a healer or alchemist shows that you know that letting people know it is magic that you work would be hazardous. The fact that you reached for a bottle rather than a gem, wand, or staff shows that you are at best a talented amateur in the mystic arts. Further evidence of that fact can be found here."

The intruder crouched behind the counter, moved a floor board, and retrieved a thick and ancient tome.

"You found this in a wizard's tower in Ravenwood. It, and some mystic paraphernalia, were all you could sniff out before you were chased out by the usual mob of angry villagers. The fact that you allowed yourself to be chased proves that you are a coward. This little scam you are running here proves something else. It isn't about helping people, because were that the goal you would have cured them. And it isn't about money, because even someone with your entry-level knowledge of magic could easily find more profitable pursuits.

"No, this little game is about power. You like holding their lives in your hand. Power is why you ventured into that tower in the first place. And I know all of this simply by paying attention . . . which means anyone else with half a mind could do the same."

"But how did you find the book!?"

"Ah, yes. That, I concede, required a measure of training. For future reference, there is a material called scatter-cloth which you ought to employ if you hope to conceal mystic items from the mystically adept."

"So you are a wizard, too."

"Yes. And in anticipation of your next question, I came with an offer. You want power? I've got a few tricks and trinkets I would be willing to give you."

"Like what?"

"Well, this, for one," said the stranger, tossing his stick in her direction.

Damona clumsily caught the staff. The instant her fingers closed about it, she could feel a power surge forth from the elegantly carved masterpiece. It was dizzying, intoxicating, a thousand times stronger than she'd ever dreamed she'd become. Just as she began to recover her senses and come to grips with her newfound might, the staff was pulled from her grasp. With it went every ounce of its power. In the wake of the veritable sea of magic, she felt like a hollow shell when reduced to her own level.

"Give it back! Give it back!" she cried desperately, clawing for it.

"Not to worry, you'll have it--and a bit of instruction to be sure you use it properly. I'll even toss in a few other items and an old pet of mine."

"What do I need to do?" she asked, eyes longingly locked on the staff.

"That wizard's tower . . . It sits on the intersection of a few minor ley lines, has some useful permanent enchantments, and every corner is stuffed with books very much like the one you've stolen. That knowledge, combined with this staff, should be enough to make you one of the most powerful sorcerers in a generation. I think you should take it back."

"I don't understand. What do you get out of all of this?"

"Well, people fear magic, but it has been so long since they've had to face it on a grand stage, I think it would be useful to remind them why they fear it."

"There must be a catch."

"A minor one. The tower has a current occupant who will need to be cleared away. A young woman--a mere girl, really--who has been fortunate enough to remain there unharassed for a few years."

"And she has been reading the books."

"Potentially, but that is at best your second concern. Foremost is the dragon. It is young, clever, and viciously dedicated to her defense."

Damona's entranced gaze was finally broken by this final point.

"A . . . a dragon. Does she control it?"

"If only she did," said the stranger. "It would be like a child trying to swing a club. No, this beast defends her of its own accord."

A conflicted look seized her features.

"And if I don't want to face this beast?"

"Then I give my gifts to a more motivated party. And before the thought even enters your mind, if you were to take my generosity and forsake the task, I would be left with no choice but to retrieve my gifts. And I can be quite justifiably forceful when I feel I have been wronged."

"So I chase the girl and the dragon away, and the tower and staff are mine."

"Damona, if you think you can simply chase a dragon away, you have much to learn about the stubbornness of such animals. And as for the girl? Well, you were once a young woman chased from the very same tower, and now look what is about to happen."

"You want me to kill them."

"I want you to have the tower so that you can put a face on the fear your people already feel. To do so, you would do well to deal with its current residents in a permanent manner."

"If you are so powerful, why aren't you taking the tower yourself? Why don't you become the force everyone fears?"

"My dear, I am already the force that everyone fears. It serves my purposes that others believe otherwise. If I were you, I would embrace that fact rather than questioning it."

"I see."

"Excellent. Then let the lessons begin . . ."

Chapter 6

Halfax and Jade stood at the edge of the ice and snow surrounding the tower. The girl's most recent interest was archery, and it was one that the dragon was eager for her to take up. Jade had learned much, and was already nearly able to take care of herself, but Halfax was still responsible for all of the hunting. Were she to learn to use a bow, she might learn to hunt for herself as well. With a bit of effort, the girl had managed to fashion a bow and some arrows based upon the description in a book about weapons of war. Now the dragon was coaching her in the proper methods of use.

Strictly speaking, Halfax didn't know how to use a bow. He'd never done so, and likely never would. He had, however, been on the wrong end of one quite often. When it is the difference between an easy escape and a painful reminder, one soon learns when an archer is aiming the bow properly.

"No, hold it with your other fingers. Hook your thumb over them," he instructed.

"Are you sure? That feels awkward," she replied, flipping through the pages of the book. "Ah, no, I see. It's called 'The Ulvard Grip.' It's supposed to help you hold it steady longer. Okay, I'll give it a try."

Jade strained at the bow, drawing back its string, and took aim at the target. After a few moments, she let the arrow fly. It hissed through the air and struck the makeshift target well off center.

"I'm getting closer! Did you see, Hal? Halfax?"

She looked to her protector. The beast had trained its eyes on a tiny, distant form in the sky.

"Is something wrong?" She asked.

"Get inside the tower, and bar all of the doors," he ordered, without taking his eyes off of the rapidly approaching form.

"What is it?"

"GET IN THE TOWER!" he roared, the crackle of fire on his breath as he flared his wings.

It had been years since she'd heard that tone of voice and seen that posture. Last time, it was because a bear had decided that she and Halfax were trespassing in its territory. Whatever that was in the sky, Halfax was certain it meant her harm, and she had never known the dragon to be wrong. She rushed back to the tower and shut the door tight, sliding the brace into place. After frantically giving the same treatment to the other entrance, she climbed the tower and watched anxiously as the form in the sky grew closer.

It was a creature that, at a glance, seemed to be a dragon. The illusion didn't last long. Its basic shape was like that of Halfax, though a bit larger, but that was where the similarity ended. In place of scales was a rough, almost stony hide, coal black. It had no eyes, only deep hollows where they should be, and rather than a mouthful of teeth, it had a serrated beak.

Jade realized that it perfectly matched the description of a monster Halfax spoke of in his nightly story, a beast he called a dragoyle. As it drew closer, Jade could see that it bore a passenger, a black-cloaked figure. Before she could make out any more details, beast and rider dipped down below the treetops, striking the ground hard enough for the frightened girl to feel it even at the top of the tower.

Halfax stalked low to the ground, keeping a dense stand of trees between himself and the intruder. He'd never faced a dragoyle before, but he'd learned much from his mother. Most of what he'd learned told him that he did not want to tangle with the beast if he didn't have to. At the moment, it had not yet noticed him, so it was of little concern. The dragon focused on the rider. Its scent was unfamiliar, a human woman. She seemed unsteady on the dragoyle's back, one hand held in a white-knuckled grip upon the edge of an ancient-looking saddle. The other hand was held low, gripping something hidden from view. He felt something about her. It was not something that he could see or smell or hear. It was a sensation deeper than that. Something powerful, ominous.

He kept pace as beast and rider crept forward, moving in a meandering path among the trees. They moved erratically, as though the rider was not fully in control of her mount. Under her inexpert guidance the beast stumbled and pitched, taking sudden steps and then overcompensating in the other direction. Cursing under her breath, the woman nearly lost her balance as the dragoyle shuffled into a tree. In raising her other hand to keep from falling, she revealed an ornately carved staff.

The sight sparked a memory deep in the dragon's mind. He knew that sensation, the force growing stronger in waves. It was magic. She was a sorceress, and for him to feel the pressure of her will at this distance, she was a powerful one. Whether the power was her own or flowing from her weapon didn't matter. The only thing that mattered was that he had no defense against magic. His thick hide could turn away arrows and swords, searing fire and icy water. His claws could cleave the thickest armor, but fighting magic was like fighting the wind. There was simply nothing for him to sink his teeth into. His only hope was to get his claws into the mystic before she could bring her strength to bear. If he could reach her before she could gather a spell, she was flesh and blood just like anyone else. She would fall.

Halfax thundered forward with a speed that would be startling even for a creature half his size. The spellcaster's head snapped toward him, genuine terror in her eyes. A panicked word, unmistakably arcane, sputtered from her lips. The dragon's eyes narrowed, his muscles tensing in preparation for an attack, but her staff remained dim. Instead, the sluggish, unguided creature she rode suddenly seemed to come alive. At the sound of what must have been a command, the monster pivoted to face the thundering dragon and opened its black maw.

A dragoyle was not born; it was constructed. A living weapon designed to utterly destroy all that it faced. As such, it was not fire that the beast breathed. That would be too clean, too brief. Instead, the creature exhaled a wretched black cloud that curled forth, sizzling and corroding everything it touched. It was nasty stuff, but slower than fire. Halfax dove aside without missing a step, drawing in breath for his own attack.

"Protect me, you blasted thing!" cried Damona desperately.

A lance of fire erupted from Halfax's mouth, but the black beast reared and the flames splashed uselessly against its stony hide. The two beasts clashed. Massive swipes of stout, vicious claws revealed that the dragoyle was stronger by far than a mere difference in size could explain. Stone shattered to pebbles and trees splintered under the force of the blows--but such power came at the cost of agility. Halfax leaped and rolled, keeping himself a hairsbreadth from being torn apart. Every spare instant was spent attempting to pull the sorceress from its back. She had yet to put her staff to use, maddened eyes locked on the dragon and petrified limbs frozen in a death grip upon her steed's harness.

Finally one of Halfax's claws came near enough to tear at her cloak. It was enough to pull her from her shocked state and push her to action.

"In the air! In the air, dammit! Get me above this thing so I can rain hell on it!" Damona ordered.

The beast did not heed until she managed to string together a sequence of awkward syllables that must have been another command. Then it extended its wings and lurched skyward, shearing the branches from the nearest trees. Rhythmic thrusts of the powerful wings filled the forest with gale-force bursts as it slowly hauled itself into the air.

Halfax dashed into the shelter of a nearby stand of trees as another dose of miasma burst from the monster's mouth and swirled chaotically in the whistling wind. A smile came to the face of the sorceress.

"Yes! Yes, run! Run!" she cried madly, raising her staff high.

In her voice, Halfax could hear a thrill, a confidence filling her to overflowing, a mad blood lust. She behaved as though she was invincible--but power wasn't everything. Experience was the difference between a deadly wizard and a dead one, and to his trained eye, Damona's inexperience was painfully clear. Her beast was strong, but it was slow and clumsy, even on the ground. Once in the air, it was all the monster could do to stay there. And she had raised her staff, the focus of her power, high into the air, making it a glaring and vulnerable target. The wings of her creature churned the air with an almost deafening roar, slicing sky and drowning out the beat of smaller wings. She began to stir the air with her weapon, voice forming twisted and otherworldly hexes. All the while, her eyes were trained at the ground, scanning the icy land below for Halfax, but he was not so foolish. He worked his wings, climbing as silently as he could until he was above her. Below, runes carved into the surface of her staff darkened. He began to dive, but a breath of wind from his wings betrayed him.

In more a panicked reflex than a mindful maneuver, Damona turned and spat a word of magic. A moment later and his jaws would have been about her. Instead, a wave of darkness launched from the staff, forcing Halfax to dive to avoid it. The more nimble dragon cut expertly through the air, evading sweeping tail, slashing claw, and crackling spell. A ball of destructive black magic wove drunkenly through the sky, arcing downward. Where the bolts of energy struck the ground, stone was shattered and trees were pulverized. A single stray attack might level the tower with Jade inside. This needed to end--now.

The noble beast grew more bold, and the wizard more desperate. Magic was taking its toll, though, and had she the mind to spare, Damona might have noticed that each blast leeched more color from her skin. Blackness was gathering around her eyes, and her nails were darkening as well. The spells were twisting her soul, draining her strength--but, as they did, her desire to strike down the dragon grew ever more intense. Fear turned to anger. How dare this beast presume to evade her? How dare it stand against her!? Her emotions were fanning the very flames that were consuming her.

"You will fall, beast! If you are too much of a coward to hold still, then I shall turn the very skies against you!"

A sequence of placeless, unnatural words began to flow from her mouth. They were no longer unsteady or clumsily phrased. Instead, they seemed to craft themselves, as though she were merely the vessel that gave them form. The incantation went to work, thickening and darkening the gray clouds above into an angry black sky. Wind whistled and howled, catching the dragon's wings awkwardly and forcing him to struggle to keep his course. Thunder rolled and lightning flashed. A rain, heavy and constant, began to hammer down from a sky that had delivered naught but snow for years.

The frigid water soaked the sorceress to the bone, but she took no notice, eyes locked on the dragon struggling fruitlessly against the hostile wind. Damona guided the gale, hauling the dragon backward. Halfax trimmed his wings and pointed his nose into it, attempting to dive through the storm and back to the ground, but the force was too much, keeping him aloft despite his best efforts. The carefully crafted air current split to avoid the dragoyle, providing the mystic with a stationary target. A fresh bolt of black magic began to form.

The dragon looked back. He was making no progress, he couldn't escape, and in moments she would release an attack easily twice the size of those that had made short work of trees moments earlier. Already he could feel the crackling power of it reaching toward him, like a ravenous attack dog straining at its leash. He couldn't wait any longer. He had to act now.

He flicked his wings backward, shifting them from a streamlined posture to great billowing sails. They caught the wind that had held him back, dragging him with it and launching him at the sorceress. A deft pivot brought his teeth and claws to bear an instant before he collided with his enemy with enough force to stagger even the massive dragoyle. His attack dug deep into the stony hide of the dragoyle and shattered the concentration that held both the wind and the bolt of magic in under Damona's control. The wave of blackness splashed against dragon and dragoyle alike, sizzling each. Halfax shrugged off the furious burning and clamped his jaws on the monster's wing.

Now caught in her own storm and entwined with a raging dragon, Damona's monstrous mount began to plummet earthward.

Fear finally cutting through her damaged confidence, the sorceress turned her maddened eyes to the rapidly approaching ground. In stirring up the skies and hurling her attacks, she had guided the dragoyle high into the sky. If she didn't stop her fall before the ground did, there was no way that she would survive. But panic was the enemy of precision, and as she fumbled through her mind for something that might be of some use, she instead settled on the one spell she could recall that she might be able to cast quickly enough to fell the dragon. She wrenched her staff free from the tangle, pointed it to the sky, and spoke the words of the spell.

Some distance away, Jade watched in terror as the spectacle high above the forest unfolded. In the darkness of the storm, she could not tell where Halfax ended and the dragoyle began, but they were both falling. She spoke a silent prayer and strained to see. Something was happening. The air around her felt tingly, and her hair was standing on end. Suddenly, the world went white. A brilliant flash of lightning split the sky, shaking the earth with the force of its thunder. The searing light burned a silhouette of the scene into her eyes. A streak of intensity traced a jagged path from clouds to forest, and passed through the distant, agonized form of her friend and protector. Tears in her eyes and anger in her heart, Jade rushed to the stairs.

A smoldering figure crashed to the earth below, tearing branches from trees. A moment later, the lurching form of the dragoyle followed suit, its rider shrieking a terrified and tortured attempt at a half a dozen different spells. She had not known that lightning was not a precise weapon, and Halfax had still been wrapped about the black beast when the bolt had struck. Charred, broken wings did little to slow the dragoyle's fall, and it struck a stand of trees with force enough to level them and turn the monster to rubble.

For a time, all was still. No longer fueled by dark will, the storm subsided, rain pattering to a stop. Smoke rose slowly from the mound of broken wood that had once been a dense patch of forest. Then came a voice, quiet and hoarse, filtering through the debris. A hand, skin white as milk and nails black as night, thrust from the pile. The fingers were clinging to the impossibly intact staff. Tendrils of energy writhed across its surface, worming along the arm and into the rubble. Fragments began to drift into the air. First one by one, then by the dozen.

A pit was excavated, and from within rose Damona--or what was left of her. Burns covered her body. Bones were shattered, limbs twisted at grotesque angles. She croaked a few more words, each accompanied by coughs and sprays of blackened blood, and the magic went to work. Bones clicked and shifted back into place. Gashes closed, burns cleared, and her voice grew stronger. In seconds, she appeared whole once more . . . but much the worse for wear. Her features were sunken and drawn, skin almost translucent, showing black veins beneath. Her vision was an indistinct mass of blue and purple blotches, and her hearing was little more than a dull whistle, lingering effects from the bolt of lightning that she had no spell to heal. She wiped blood from the corner of her mouth, turning her gaze to the broken trees and the broken dragon that lay among them.

She raised her left hand high above her head, grip tight about the staff. Arcane words began to slip from her lips, conjuring forth a swirling darkness above her raised fingers. The gleam in her eye was maniacal. Each syllable caused the churning, crackling ball of black energy to swell. The dragon was already a motionless wreck, but she would leave nothing to chance. She would leave nothing at all.

When she was satisfied with its intensity, Damona made ready to release the vicious mass of magic. Suddenly, a hissing sound cut the air, an arrow slicing across the wizard's arm. The pain was sudden and sharp enough to pull her mind from its task. Without concentration to maintain it, the spell scattered and dissipated, trailing long ebony streamers that withered and blackened all that they touched.

The injured spellcaster turned, fury in her eyes, to see Jade run desperately for the shelter of a nearby tree. Damona waved the staff over the wound. In seconds, it boiled away until only a thin black line remained. The grin on her face widened.

"I'm glad you left the tower, child. I was afraid I might damage it while looking for you. Now come here. This will be easier for you if you cooperate."

Jade stepped from behind the tree and released another arrow. Damona spat a syllable and thrust the staff aside. A wave of force swept through the forest, deflecting the arrow, knocking Jade to the ground, and snapping away the smallest branches of a dozen trees.

"I won't tell you again. Hold still and I'll be gentle and quick. Do something stupid like run or fire another arrow and you'll twist and burn."

Jade struggled to her feet and fumbled for another arrow, but the force had torn them all away. She raised her gaze to the wizard. Her eyes darted upward briefly before opening wide as saucers. In a sprawling motion, she dropped to the ground, hands covering her head.

"That's a good girl. Just hold--"

Had the thunder not left her near deaf, she might have heard the crackle of broken trees being forced aside. Instead, Damona's first warning was a flare of light. Her second was a rush of heat. There was no time for a third.

Flames rushed about her form before a word of magic could be spoken. A half-dozen spells designed to protect her shattered beneath the might of a direct blast of dragon's fire. In an instant, without so much as a gasp of pain, Damona was no more.

Jade raised her head to see a smoldering crater where once the sorceress had been. There was no trace of humanity left in the blackened, steaming ground. As her eyes crept upward, she saw Halfax. She felt as though someone had torn the heart from her body. The lightning had fairly split him in two, a jagged red slice running from snout to tail along his right side and across his eye. Blood poured along the length of the sizzling wound. Both wings were shredded tatters, and his jaw and one foreleg were horribly crooked. Whatever strength had allowed him to haul himself free for this final attack was draining away. Finally, he collapsed on his left side.

Jade rushed to him, tears in her eyes. Every fiber of her being wanted her to cradle Halfax's head in her arms. She wanted to beg him to be all right, to pray that he could be saved. Had she been any other girl, perhaps she would have. But Halfax had spent as much time raising her as her own parents, and she had learned much from him. She'd learned that if you needed something, you learned how to get it. If you couldn't afford to lose something, you did what it took to keep it safe.

"Hal! Halfax, listen to me!" she cried out, tears in her eyes. "I need you to open your eyes! Listen to me!"

The beast's eyelid wavered slightly.

"Listen!" she cried, slapping the dragon and very nearly gashing her hand in the process.

His one healthy eye pulled slowly open and focused weakly upon her.

"Halfax, focus on me! Stay focused! I can help you! I am going to the tower to get some things and I am going to fix you right up, okay!?" she shouted as the tears ran down her cheeks. "I just need you to keep your eyes open, do you understand? Just keep breathing. I'll do the rest!"

With that, Jade sprinted back to the tower and grabbed as much as she could carry, lugging bulging bags and clanking tools back to the dragon's side. The beast was still breathing, but only just. There was no time to lose, so she set immediately about her task.

There were only a handful of humans in the world who knew anything about how to treat a dragon's wounds, and none had written any of the books in the tower. Jade knew a great deal about healing humans, though, and other animals as well. Many of the books had been devoted to those subjects. What's more, having spent most of her life beside Halfax had brought her a great deal of knowledge about his kind. She had all of the pieces, then. She just had to hope that she could find the right way to put them together before it was too late.

Blankets and rope became makeshift bandages on a dragon's scale. She'd seen him sear minor cuts closed with a burst of flame. The edge of a kitchen knife heated over a hastily built fire did the same job. For wounds too wide to be similarly sealed, strips of sinew and techniques learned from a book about leather armor repair did for a dragon what needle and thread would do for a person. Long, stout branches became splints, and all of the strength she could muster managed to set broken bones. Mixtures of herbs and extracts were poured down his throat in doses dozens of times stronger than the recipes recommended. It was an ordeal, lasting hours, but Jade worked tirelessly. Not until her resources were completely depleted did she relent, well into the night.

She placed her weary head on the beast's chest. A weak but steady heartbeat greeted her. Jade took a step back. Halfax's potent blood stung at her hands and stained every inch of her clothes. Without her purpose to sustain her, all of the exhaustion she'd managed to push aside came down upon her at once. She lowered herself to the icy ground, leaned against her deeply sleeping protector, and made ready to close her eyes.

Motion at the edge of the fire's light jarred her eyes open again. She knew the forest was a place of struggle, a place of predators and prey. For the woodland hunters, the scent of blood was like an alarm bell. If it was the blood of small creature, it meant an easy meal; the blood of a larger predator meant much more. Wild creatures understood competition, and she knew that they all would know that a fallen dragon, if it could be kept from rising, meant more meat for all.

It was not one form but many; several sets of fiery yellow eyes gleamed in the flickering light. Wolves, eager to take Halfax's place for themselves, were gathering. Jade crept to the flames, pulled free a burning branch, and planted herself beside her friend. The dragon had pushed himself beyond the limit to keep her safe. She owed it to him to do the same.

Chapter 7

"Hal? Hal?" Jade's wavering voice was pleading.

The dragon's good eye opened. He was wracked by sharp, constant pain, but he was alive. Inches in front of his face was Jade. She looked dead on her feet, and she was shivering violently from the cold, but seeing her friend awake brought a brief spark of joy.

"Don't try to talk. Your jaw was broken, so I had to tie it shut. I think . . . I think two of your legs are broken, too, but . . . can you stand? We need to get back to the tower."

Halfax painfully raised his head. The light of the rising sun revealed the remnants of Jade's hellish night. All around them, the snow was littered with paw prints. Here and there, charred branches lay discarded. The dragon could only imagine what sort of experience the girl had been through, but he could learn of it later. For now, Jade was right. They needed shelter.

Amid growls and groans of pain, Halfax struggled to his feet. Wooden splints creaked, bandaged wounds trickled blood, and ropes strained, but he managed to stand. Together, the dragon limped and the girl trudged back to the tower. Once there, each collapsed into a long, necessary slumber.

#

The time that followed was difficult. Halfax could barely walk, and received a stern reprimand from Jade whenever he tried. That left her to provide all of the food for both of them. The young girl fortunately became an able hunter in very short order, having seen him do it so often, but even with her well-stocked garden to supplement her own meals, there were times when food had to be rationed. Without Halfax to ride to and from town, and with neither willing to consider leaving the other for long enough for her to make the journey on foot, certain supplies began to run low.

Soon, all her waking moments were filled with hunting, gardening, fashioning arrows, and preparing traps for the next day's hunt. What little time was left to spare was spent scrutinizing the books of the tower. Many of them were dedicated to healing, and she hungrily devoured every hint of a treatment that might lead Halfax to a swifter and more complete recovery. Unfortunately she had exhausted all that the impressive library had to say on the subject of conventional remedies. There were volumes more to read, but all dealt with "white magic."

Jade was dedicated to doing all she could to help her friend, but the thought of even attempting to cast a spell was terrifying to her. Halfax had warned over and over again that magic was for those trained to use it. It wasn't evil or good, but it could do terrible things if used improperly. That didn't change the fact the Halfax's wings would never heal on their own, and no amount of time would give him the sight back in his right eye. In defending her, he had paid a terrible price. She had to repay him somehow.

#

A rattle shook the whole of the tower. Jade was jarred awake--first startled, then disappointed. By the time she'd reached the door of Halfax's stable, he was only just getting to his feet again.

"What are you doing?" Jade scolded.

"It will be dawn soon. I need to hunt," he said without looking, limping painfully toward the forest.

"It sounded like a herd of elephants when you tried to stand up. I hope you don't expect to sneak up on anything," she said, walking alongside him, "and I don't think you'll be chasing anything down either. Go lie down. If you want food, I'll get you something."

Halfax continued walking.

"You'll never lose that limp if you don't give your bones some rest. You shouldn't even be talking. That jaw still looks horribly swollen."

"It is fine," he grunted.

In response, Jade prodded it with a finger. The beast jerked away with a hiss of pain.

"Clearly," she said. "You know, Halfax, I can remember a time when the idea of you telling a lie would have been unthinkable. What is this all about?"

The dragon sat heavily.

"If you were not here, I would have to do this alone. I need to be able to fend for myself."

"Hal, if I wasn't here, this never would have happened to you. And if you weren't here, I wouldn't even be alive. You've saved my life so many times, and you've taken care of me for so long, it is only right that I return the favor."

"You shouldn't have to do this. It isn't the way it is supposed to be."

"I don't have to do this, Hal. I'm doing it because I want to. Look at me, Halfax. Do you understand?"

Halfax merely stared at her.

"That's not what's wrong, is it?" she said, slowly realizing. "It isn't that I need to do it for you. It is that you *need me* to do it for you. That's it, isn't it?"

"For hundreds and hundreds of years it has been the same. I am the protector. Generation after generation. Choose the strongest, or the youngest, or the only child. Keep it safe. It is what I *am*. It was all I was ever meant to be. I stand between you and your enemies. That is how it had always been before you. Then I found you, and I had to feed you. Comfort you. I had to protect your feelings. It was not enough to make you safe, I had to make you *feel* safe. And now . . . now you feed me? You protect me? That is not how it is supposed to be!”

He stomped a healthy leg with enough force to shake snow from trees at the edge of the clearing.

“Maybe not for dragons, but that is exactly how it works for humans. First parents take care of children, then children take care of the parents. That's family.”

“I am not family.”

Jade smiled and pulled the dragon's head close, kissing him lightly on the snout.

“You are to me, Hal,” she said softly. Then, with a slap to the head and a point to the stable, she added, “Now go lay down and I'll catch you some breakfast!”

#

Jade put down the day's kill. It had taken more time than usual to bring it back. The sun was still high in the sky, but there was much to do. As she gathered her tools to prepare the food, her eyes turned to Halfax. The beast was anything but emotional, and what little he felt seldom showed on his face. To the trained eye, though, it was just as simple to determine his disposition as that of anyone else. Right now he looked defeated, forlorn. It wasn't until his injury that it had become clear how important it was to Halfax that he be useful. His purpose defined him, it was what drove him. Until his strength returned, though, as far as he was concerned, he was little more than a burden. The sense of worthlessness had robbed him of his appetite. He barely even moved, save one attempt early each morning to see if his bones would allow him either the stealth or speed to hunt and defend once more.

Jade thought hard. She needed to find something to make him feel useful until he was himself again. Slowly, a thought arose.

“Halfax. Go like this,” Jade said, twiddling the fingers on one hand.

After a moment, he imitated.

“No, with your bad paw.”

Again he attempted the motion. It was a pale imitation this time, his smallest claw failing to move at all.

“Does that hurt?” she asked.

“No,” he lied.

“Well, it looks like you've lost some . . .” she began, searching her memory for the correct word. “Dexterity. Remember when I was a little girl and you had to cut up my meat for me?”

“Yes,” he said.

Jade picked up the doe she'd brought back and dropped it in front of him.

“Separate it. And try to use your bad paw as much as possible,” she said.

Halfax glared at her briefly, then dragged the kill closer and went to work. As he did, Jade tended to the garden. She peeked briefly in his direction periodically to see him diligently at work. By the time she'd weeded and selected some ripe vegetables, he had managed to do a remarkably good job of butchering the beast.

"Good. Now reach inside and grab that big pot . . ."

Task by task, she walked Halfax through fetching wood from the pile, filling the pot from the stream, and placing the right meats and vegetables inside. Each step was of little effort for him. Seldom did he even need to stand. Many, though, required finer manipulation than he'd done in weeks. The fire was lit, and the food was cooked until the smell and tenderness was right. It took hours, but while it cooked and Halfax watched, Jade worked through the rest of the day's activities. Finally, she sampled the result. It was a trifle plain, and the vegetables were more mashed than cut, but it was actually quite good.

"There. It may not be the way you are accustomed to, but you just fetched me dinner," she said.

"This is foolish," he grumbled.

"Nonsense, it is a great help. And if you are going to mope around like a kicked puppy until you are healed up, I've got to find something for you to do. So this is your new job every day until you are back on your feet."

#

In a dark room, somewhere far away, a tall, lean figure sat in deep thought. It was the elf, the mysterious stranger who had been haunting Jade's life for all of these years. The same puzzle had occupied his mind for all of that time.

"The lucky ones," he murmured, "so very difficult to deal with."

He tapped his foot absentmindedly and stroked his chin.

"Three bloodlines left that I know of . . . can't seem to eliminate those two. That luck turns things to their favor. I need to whittle that number down. Find some way to turn good luck for her into bad luck for the world. A scenario where the best case for her is still a win for me . . ."

Slowly, a grin came to his face, as devious and malicious as the thought that inspired it.

"That could work . . ."

#

In time, Halfax mostly recovered. The strength returned to his injured legs. He resumed hunting--though, as she had developed a fondness for it, Jade now frequently accompanied him. Likewise, though it was no longer strictly necessary, Halfax aided in preparing meals and other more human chores. Working with his "hands" was more challenging than he'd expected, revealing a weakness he'd not realized he'd had. Halfax was a creature who would never pass up a chance to correct a flaw.

More than two years passed. The girl and the dragon were mercifully left alone in that time. Jade's only contact with anyone aside from Halfax came in the form of trips to the nearest town. Now that she was just past eighteen years of age, appearing alone in town did not cause nearly the stir it had when she was a child. That was not to say that she went without notice, but now it was for an entirely new set of reasons.

Their undisturbed time was no doubt largely due to Jade's remarkable--indeed, supernatural--luck. Peace was hardly the only benefit that it had afforded her, though. Perhaps the purest form taken by her extraordinary good fortune was obvious to all who saw her. She had blossomed into a woman as effortlessly and flawlessly beautiful as anyone was likely to see. Long, raven hair was kept in a meticulous braid. The simple clothes she made with her own hands shamed the work of tailors the world over by simple virtue of the exquisite form upon which they were draped. Her visits were well remembered by the men of the village, and sourly dreaded by the women. Many the young buck had attempted to court her, but all were politely turned away. The more persistent and less mannerly among them quickly learned that though she might look delicate, a dragon did not raise this young woman to be timid.

She'd managed to find a way to pay Halfax back for the gold she'd had to spend as well. The skills she'd learned in her quest to heal him, it turned out, were quite sought after within the town. Potions and powders that she concocted to cure common maladies sold as quickly as she could make them. This was partially because it hadn't occurred to her to charge much more than they cost to make, so they were substantially cheaper than those sold by traveling merchants. Mostly, though, they sold because, unlike most of what the merchants sold, they actually worked. Pain was eased, infections subsided, rashes cleared. When she was in town she tended to the more troublesome ailments personally. Before long, she found herself making trips every few weeks whether she needed goods or not, simply to sell her wares and render her services.

Always, though, she returned home to the tower and to Halfax. Her budding skill as a healer had restored his health to beyond what it had been prior to his clash with the wizard, but some injuries lingered that neither time nor traditional medicine could cure. The slash left by the lightning was now a narrow white scar running from his snout to his tail, crossing both eye and wing on the right side. Both wings were still utterly ruined, tattered shreds on a framework of crooked bones. The eye had healed to a milky white, sightless orb.

It was this latter injury that had proven most difficult for Halfax to overcome, and it was this one Jade was most dedicated to curing. Alas, she could only work with what was available. Jade simply didn't have the resources to restore her friend. All that she could do was keep learning, keep searching, hope that in time the pieces would com together.

Chapter 8

"Hal! This way!" she called out.

The pair were making their way through a patch of forest near the mountains. A handful of the more useful herbs she used in her potions grew best in the thinner air and rockier soil, so she kept a small garden near the tree line. As they made their way back, something caught Jade's eye.

"What?" Halfax asked making his way to her side.

"Do you know what this is!?" she cried eagerly.

"No."

"Aiur," she said, "It is supposed to grow only on South Crescent!"

South Crescent was a continent half of a world away, and its residents kept very much to themselves. Jade had long ago abandoned any hope of attaining resources native to that land, yet here she found a plant more precious to her than gold. She crouched and carefully took a cutting.

"Come on! Back to the tower!" she urged, fairly leaping to his back.

"Is it important?" Halfax asked.

"Right now there is nothing that matters more to me! Quickly, quickly!"

Halfax sprinted to the east. In no time at all, they reached the tower. Jade dove from the dragon's back and scrambled inside. As Halfax heaved great breaths, recovering slowly from the run, she rummaged through mounds of books. It had been more than a year since she'd last read it, but still she remembered the very page she needed. How could she forget? It was precisely what she needed, yet just out of reach for so long.

She pulled the proper book from the pile and flipped it open. It was in a different tongue, one Halfax had taught her. He hadn't known the name of the language, only that it was from South Crescent. The words at the top of the page brought tears to her eyes. "Sight from darkness . . ."

She gathered the necessary materials, cut a tiny sliver of the aiur leaf, and planted the rest in a small pot. A potent and foul-smelling brew was prepared, the precious leaf as the final ingredient. Decanting the finished concoction, she hurried outside.

"What was that all about?" Halfax muttered.

"Show me your eye," she said, excitement spilling from her voice.

He angled his massive amber-gold eye closer to her.

"No, the bad one!"

Hesitantly, and with more than a little suspicion, he turned his head to reveal the useless white eye.

"Lay your head on the ground," she said.

"Another remedy? This is foolish," he said, turning his good eye to her again.

"What? Are you afraid it will hurt? A big strong dragon like you?"

"Don't try to manipulate me," he said sternly.

"Fine. No tricks. Don't do it to prove you aren't afraid, do it because I asked you to."

With the customary sigh, Halfax lowered his head to the ground. Jade quickly straddled his neck.

"Now try to hold still. This will probably hurt . . . a lot," she said, lifting the eyelid gently and pouring in the mixture.

She could feel the beast's neck tense under her, but ever stoic, Halfax released only the merest grunt in response to what must have been a terribly painful experience.

"Now keep the eye closed," she said, reaching into her cloak as quietly as possible to retrieve an item she knew would not be well-received.

She pulled an amulet from her pocket. It was brass, heavily tarnished, and bore a pale blue gem at its center. Attached to it was a fine chain of the same metal. When the final links of the chain tugged free, they made the tiniest clink.

"What is that sound?" Halfax rumbled, his good eye shooting open.

Jade placed the amulet over the treated eye and spoke three words in a very deliberate and carefully practiced manner. A sharp growl shook Halfax and his head shot up, taking Jade with it.

"Magic?" he barked. "What are you doing speaking words of magic!?"

"I've practiced, Hal. I know precisely what I am doing," she assured, holding tight to her perch upon his neck and quietly repeating the words.

Halfax curled his neck and coiled his tail about Jade's middle, gently tugging her free.

"The treatment comes from the mixture. The magic words just make it permanent," she defended, dangling from his tail.

"I don't care. You have not been trained, you have never heard those words spoken, and you do not know if you've said them correctly. What if--"

His voice trailed off as the offending eye slid open.

"Well?" she asked hopefully.

Halfax's tail loosened, dropping Jade to the ground. He swept his head around, sampling the sights of the tower as if for the first time. The brightness at the edge of the clearing, the drifting of bees among the garden . . . For the first time in years, he was seeing them as he was meant to.

"It worked didn't it? It *worked!*" she exclaimed.

She ran to him, tears streaming down her face, and wrapped her arms tight around his neck. Halfax placed a paw behind her back and pulled her closer.

"I've been waiting so long to make it up to you. And I swear, if it is in my power, I'll give you your wings back, too," she said, releasing her embrace and wiping the tears from her cheeks. "Now, the eye isn't going to be exactly how it was. According to the spell book, this was created by dwarfs to help them navigate caves. The eye shouldn't need any light at all to see, but it won't be able to see quite as far even in daylight."

A sound in the bushes drew Halfax's attention. He released her and bolted toward it. Jade didn't need to be told why. The loss of an eye had been an enormous handicap to his hunting, one that it had taken him months to overcome. Now that he had some measure of his full vision back, no one could blame him if he was eager to put it to use. Tonight there would be a feast.

#

Far to the north, in an exquisite and well-kept room, a well-dressed man waited. His eyes turned to the door as it opened, a stately servant stepping through.

"You may have your audience with the prince now," declared the steward.

"Thank you," said the tall, all-too-familiar elf.

He stood and was led into a large, lavishly furnished parlor. Inside was an unimpressive figure in very impressive garb. His build was lean, trending toward lanky, and his expression was a pale imitation of authority. He was a man, perhaps twenty years old, who might be considered handsome if his features or posture could muster even an ounce of confidence. Instead, his bearing and presence spoke quietly of meekness, weakness, and insignificance.

"Oh, yes, and you are?" asked the prince.

"A concerned party," said the stranger.

"Er. Is that all? Generally, the steward presents my visitors with their full title and point of business," he said, brow furrowed slightly.

"Yes, well, I rather doubt your servant knew my name *or* my business. Were you to call him in here, in fact, I suspect he would be quite confused to find me in the room."

"I . . . I don't understand."

"That is hardly a surprise, Your Highness. You are Terrilius Croyden Lumineblade, latest in the impressively long, and astoundingly unbroken, Lumineblade dynasty. That should make you a towering figure in the hearts and minds of your people. Instead, you are known, you should be aware, as the frail whelp that might someday rule Vulcrest."

"Now that simply isn't true, my people love--"

"Your people are ashamed of you. Your skill with a sword is barely average, your riding skill is virtually nonexistent, and you have the force and presence of a damp washing cloth. Your people dread the day your father will die to leave the kingdom in your hands, and there are no less than seven assorted lords and knights actively contesting your claim to the crown."

"I don't have to take that from you!"

"No, you don't, and yet you are. The very fact my head is still on my shoulders says all that needs to be said about you. A stranger in the castle unannounced? Someone in your position should have called in the guards in a heartbeat. You lack any of the distinguishing qualities of a king, save birthright. In short, Your Highness, unless you are able to illustrate that you have the wisdom, the strength, and the will to lead, then this kingdom will never be yours."

"I . . . I cannot . . ."

"Not to worry. Wisdom can be provided by advisers, and strength by armies. You need only prove that you have the will, and that is simple enough. Take swift, decisive action in the protection of your land and your people will see in you a leader."

"What would you suggest?"

"Do you recall, some years ago, when a dark sorceress emerged from Tressor and rode a dragon creature into the heart of Ravenwood?"

"Of course. It was the day of that terrible storm. My father forbade any to venture far into Ravenwood because of it."

"Well, Ravenwood is the finest hunting ground on the continent. Losing it is a tremendous hardship. And to react to a threat within your own borders by simply ignoring it? Is that truly the act of a leader?"

The prince's eyes drifted, seeming to focus on a point beyond the walls of the room.

"The wizard and her beast must be destroyed . . ." he said vaguely.

"Very wise idea, Your Highness. I happen to know that they have taken refuge in a wizard's tower deep within the forest."

"I am quite aware of Ravenwood's tower."

"Splendid. So you know where they are, and you know that she must be killed. Now, if you were to order me to, I believe I could be coerced into performing this deed personally."

"No."

"No?"

"I am the prince, and, as you say, I am the one with something to prove. I shall gather the best of our soldiers, I shall lead them into Ravenwood, and I shall defeat the sorceress myself."

"Will you, now? Then perhaps you would consider including me in your party. I--"

"No. I do not know who you are, sir, and though you may think me a fool, I am not so blind as to mistake a wolf for a sheep. You are after something. I thank you for stepping forward to inform me of my shortcomings. There are few willing to speak to royalty so frankly. And I thank you for inspiring me to take action for the benefit of my kingdom, but whatever plan you mean to hatch, you shall not. So leave me. I've much to prepare."

"As you wish, Your Highness," replied the stranger.

He excused himself, walking out of the prince's chambers amid various looks of confusion and concern. Indeed, no one remembered allowing him in, but the fact that he was inside and seemed to fit so comfortably into the castle atmosphere led each to assume that he had been invited by another.

"Not the ideal outcome," the stranger mused aloud to no one, "but it will do. The boy knows nothing of battle, and yet acts as though he is invincible, as though making the decision was the only challenge. One way or another, that will ensure at least one of the targets will be destroyed."

#

Some days later, Halfax was stalking through the forest on his daily patrol. Years without being disturbed had not dulled the edge of his dedication. For a dragon, a few years was barely the blink of an eye. He looked and listened, but for the most part, he replied upon his nose. The forest was dense with scent. The crisp smell of fresh snow, the distant aroma of ripe vegetables in Jade's clearing, and the enticing scent of a deer all wafted on the same breeze from the west. The dragon had taken a few stealthy steps toward his would-be prey when a northern gust of wind carried with it a mixture of smells that set off alarms in his mind. Horses and men. Many of each. Halfax burst into a sprint, heading directly for the source of the wind.

As he drew nearer, the sound of hooves and the clink and jingle of armor confirmed his fears. Soldiers. More than a dozen of them. Before long, they were in sight. Halfax could determine their intentions with little more than a glance. Each was armed with heavy, cruel weapons. Oversized axes, spiked clubs, two-handed swords, and longbows. Things capable of piercing armor . . . or scales. They were dragonslayers, or hoped to be. The undeniable looks of anxiety on their faces suggested they had little experience in the area, and no confidence. Only the man in the center of the group stood as an exception. In place of anxiety was a look of determination. He alone was armed with a light sword, and the higher quality of his ornate armor labeled him as their superior, in title if not in skill.

The horses, more mindful of hidden threats than their riders, became uneasy. Most of the men were able to quickly set their steeds straight again. The well-dressed leader had more difficulty. When he finally succeeded, he felt the gaze of his men. It was the prince, and alone among his men for the first time in ages, it was only now becoming clear to him the contempt they felt. Drawing himself with as much regal bearing as he could muster, he spoke.

"Right, Commander," he said, "the horses seem restless. How much further until we reach the tower?"

Halfax's expression sharpened.

"Not long. Within the hour, Your Highness," replied the soldier.

He hissed the prince's title like a profanity, a subtlety the noble failed to notice.

"Good, excellent. And we are all prepared to put this woman and her pet to a swift and certain end?" he asked.

"Yes, Your Highness. As prepared as any men can be."

That was all that Halfax needed to hear. If they were planning to attack Jade, then they would go no further. The dragon readied himself. He'd dealt with dragonslayers before. Perhaps they claimed to do what they did for the good of their country or for the vast rewards, but there was always a deeper desire: glory. These men wanted a reputation. They wanted to prove to themselves that they were strong enough to stand against this mighty beast. The way to deal with them was not to kill them. That would only bring more men to replace them, better armed and more determined. No, one must fulfill their expectations. Give them what they wanted. Terrify them, clash with them. Give them scars to show off and stories to tell around the campfire. Give them a fight they would never forget, and one that they would never want to repeat.

With a slow, purposeful step, Halfax snapped a branch on the ground. The men turned toward the sound in perfect unison. He plodded slowly toward them, crushing brush and stomping the earth. Were he trying to kill these men, he would never be so clumsy in his approach, but in the mind of a man, a dragon was a mindless monster thrashing through the forest. It was best not to disappoint. His approach ratcheted the tension tighter than the bow strings that the archers shakily held ready. He let out a low growl that shook the trees and seemed to come from everywhere at once.

At the sound, the horses panicked, forcing the soldiers to struggle to keep them under control. Some had more success than others. The well-dressed and poorly-equipped prince failed completely, his horse breaking formation and galloping madly away amid his angry protests. Halfax chose that moment to reveal himself, broken wings spread and thrashing, teeth bared and gleaming, and a bloodcurdling roar splitting the air. The bowmen released their arrows, not a single one even close to hitting its target. The sight of the charging monster was too much for half of the men, sending them galloping back from whence they came. The more steadfast of the men abandoned their horses and raised their weapons, ready to do battle.

The battle that followed was as well-choreographed as a dance. Halfax darted in and lashed with claw and tail, separating the warriors into manageable groups. Most of the archers were gone, but those who remained each got a skillfully aimed burst of flame, just strong enough to snap the bowstring and singe some skin. That left only the heavy weapons, which were little threat at all. The well-earned reputation of invincibility that dragons enjoyed was thanks in no small part to the fact that most weapons powerful enough to do any damage were far too slow to be any good. By the time a suitably large ax was raised and ready, Halfax had easily put the wielder on his back with a firm butt of his head or a careful rake of his claws. The broadswords were a bit faster, but exhausting to use. One or two soldiers hacked a shallow notch into his scales--one even drew blood--but by the third swing, no man among them had the strength to manage anything more than a glancing blow.

In no time at all, each of the men had taken more than he could stand. One by one, they retreated. The final warrior to go was the commander. He was tired and bloodied, but he refused to back away until his sword, a weapon even more battle-scarred than he, broke upon the dragon's back. Finally, he'd had enough. He moved as quickly as his tired body could manage in the direction the others had gone, hand still clutching the broken sword. Halfax gave chase for a few steps, and heaved a blast of flame for good measure. As quickly as it had begun, it was over.

The beast allowed himself a brief moment of pride, but it flickered away as the sound of frantic hoofbeats began to approach again. From among the trees came the prince. He had managed to get some degree of control over his steed again and was urging it back into the battleground. Halfax planted his feet, drew in a breath, and unleashed a rush of flame. He'd intended it to startle the horse beyond any hope of regaining control and he was, if anything, *too* successful. The terrified animal thrashed about, turning abruptly enough to hurl the prince from its back. In a hapless tumble of flailing limbs and gleaming armor, he careened toward a tree. A dull thud and a rush of pained breath marked his impact. He fairly wrapped around the trunk before recoiling and tumbling to the ground. Halfax continued on his way, leaving the man wheezing and attempting to reclaim the wind that had been knocked from him.

"You . . . you come back here!" he managed, crawling after the dragon, "Damn you, beast! Face me!"

The would-be king struggled to his feet, leaning heavily on the tree.

"You are a . . . blight on my people! We have been deprived of a valuable hunting ground, a lifeline, by . . . you and your dark sorceress of a master! I swear to all that will hear me that I shall reclaim it for my people. Even if I have to strike you down myself! Even if I have to strike *her* down mys--"

He never managed to finish the oath. A sweeping swat of a claw sent him first to the tree, then to the ground. Halfax stood over the now-motionless noble, feeling for a moment as though what had just happened had nothing to do with him. The suggestion that this man would harm Jade robbed him of centuries of carefully cultivated control, allowing a flash of raw anger to take hold for an instant. The result was the crumbled, broken wreck of a human being before him.

The dragon scolded himself. Killing a prince . . . they would have to leave now. Killing a prince would bring the wrath of a kingdom. He plodded slowly away, but as he did, a nagging sensation that he couldn't place began to make its voice heard. It reminded him of the sense he had used to find Jade all of those years ago. It wasn't something of the body; it was something of the mind, of the spirit. A weak, subtle glow just beyond the point of vision. An aura that only people like Jade shared . . . people who were of a Chosen line . . .

Halfax turned and rushed back to the fallen prince. It was unmistakable now, glaringly obvious. The aura was not a match for Jade's, but it had the same quality, the same power. This man was of a Chosen bloodline, and a familiar one. It was the one his brother had been tasked with protecting . . . and now he had severed that line . . .

Prince Lumineblade coughed weakly. The dragon leaned low over the injured noble. The fall from the horse and the one savage attack had not quite been enough to kill him, but death was near. There was too much blood too quickly. He would not survive the night without treatment. He might not survive the hour. There was no other choice, and no time to lose. Halfax scooped up the ailing prince and ran with all of the speed he could muster toward the tower.

Outside the tower, under the warm sun of its perpetual spring, Jade was tending to her garden when she heard the thundering return of her friend.

"Hal," she began without looking, "what was all of that noise? I thought I heard--what happened to you!?"

She ran to the winded dragon. The handful of places where swords had met their mark oozed blood. None of the wounds were serious, a fact that mattered little to Jade, who was so distracted by the injuries, it took her a moment to notice the cargo Halfax carried.

"Did this man do this to you?" she hissed.

"He and his men. You must help him."

"Why should I? Did you do anything to deserve those gashes you've got?"

"I defended myself--and you."

"Then he got what he deserved. Drop him somewhere and let me look at those wounds."

"You must help him. He is from a Chosen bloodline."

"A Chosen blood . . . like me? Is he a member of my family?" she asked, a gleam of hope in her eye.

"No. He smells like those my brother Windsor was protecting."

"Windsor . . ." Jade said, thinking back to the stories of her youth. "Windsor was protecting the Lumineblades. So this is royalty . . ."

She looked over the ailing human. His wounds were many, and more than one of them would take his life if given the time. Her eyes then turned to the dragon. After the events with Damona, Jade had become very protective of Halfax, and slow to trust others. Her mind told her this was another enemy, come to hurt her and her dear friend. Her heart, though, demanded she do what she could to help. And besides, this *was* almost certainly a noble. If he didn't come back, there would be more to find him.

"Fine. Put him inside. I'll fix him up and send him on his way," she said finally.

The dragon clutched the young man in the claws of one paw and reached through the doorway, placing him gently on the floor. Immediately, she set to work. Ointments and salves were applied. Clothes were removed to better access the injuries. Wide gashes were stitched, small ones bandaged. It took some time, even with her practiced hand. By the time she'd taken care of the urgent wounds, Halfax had seared his own injuries shut, leaving the injured noble as her only concern. Worse, the man seemed to have developed a fever, and had lost considerably more blood than she'd thought.

Hours passed. Jade placed a wet cloth on his head, cleaned away dried blood, and did all of the other things healers do when it is out of their hands.

As she did, she looked over him. Surely this was not the face of a man who would hunt a dragon for sport. His face, even at rest, had a look of intelligence, and a grace that betrayed a dash of elf in his ancestry. That made sense. If he was a part of the Lumineblade dynasty then, according to Halfax, Desmeres Lumineblade and Trigorah Teloran were at the root of his family tree. Each was an elf, at least in part.

Whatever its heritage, it was a handsome face. As she admired her visitor, he began to stir. She stood and began to prepare for when he would wake.

Chapter 9

Before long, the prince opened his eyes. He did not recognize his surroundings. Beneath him was a simple cot. A cluttered cottage surrounded him, the smell of simmering food heavy in the air. Outside the window, the golden rays of the setting sun fell upon an apple tree ready for harvest, yet beyond that were snow-covered pines. At the sound of footsteps, he turned to a woman, radiant in her beauty, holding a steaming bowl of broth.

"Speak," the girl demanded.

"I have died. This is paradise," he murmured.

"Not quite, I'm afraid. Though it wasn't for lack of trying," Jade said, handing him the bowl. "Drink."

The prince accepted the bowl and put it to his lips, the warm, delicious meal trickling down his throat. The fog of sleep cleared, and the memories of his last moments of consciousness returned.

"I remember now. I fought a dragon . . ." he said.

"Yes. You did," Jade said bitterly.

"Where are my men?" he asked.

"I wouldn't know."

He glanced down.

"Where are my clothes?" he asked, suddenly realizing the state he was in.

"In a bloody pile on the ground," she said, gesturing in their direction, "just like you were a few hours ago."

"You undressed me!?" he exclaimed, somewhere between shocked and mortified.

"It was that or let you bleed to death," she replied simply.

He lifted the blanket and quickly lowered it again.

"You *completely* undressed me!?"

"There was a nasty puncture on your thigh. I'm a healer. You haven't got anything I haven't seen before."

"M-my dear girl, I am a very--you shouldn't--"

"You're blushing," she said with a grin.

When she'd first learned of what he'd done to Halfax, Jade had been furious at this man. When she saw what state he was in, sympathy overcame her, then concern. Now that he was through the woods, she'd prepared herself for anger again, but something about his flustered stammering was almost endearing.

"Do you know who I am, miss?" he finally managed.

"Roughly. One of the Lumineblades, right? A lord or some such."

"I am a pr--*the* prince, miss. Soon to be king!"

"I see," she said, unimpressed.

Halfax had taught Jade much, and the many books had taught her more, but nothing had taught her the finer points of social grace. To her, the prince was just another patient, and an uncooperative one at that. When he tried to rise, blanket wrapped tight about him, she firmly pushed him back to the cot.

"Lay down. You aren't getting up until I am satisfied you have recovered enough. Eat your soup and I will look you over."

She placed a hand on his head, and one by one began to investigate the wounds she'd had to treat. He drank desperately of the contents of the bowl, partially because he was famished, but mostly because he hoped to finish quickly enough to prevent her from asking to peek under the . . .

"That will be quite unnecessary!" he sputtered as she reached for the blanket, "You've done more than enough, miss."

"You need to stop calling me miss," she replied, fetching a strong-smelling paste and leaning close to apply it to a cut on his head. "What is your name?"

"I am Prince Terrilius Croyden Lumineblade III."

"Well, Terry, I--"

"Terrilius! Err, Prince Ter--no, Prince Lumin . . ." he stammered, pausing to gently push her away and gather himself before continuing. "The proper style of address for someone in my position is 'Your Highness.'"

"Your position right now is convalescing in a bed in my home. Naked. I'd say that hardly calls for courtly formalities. Now, my name is Jade Rinton. You can call me Jade."

"I . . . yes, well, I suppose that, under the circumstances, a more casual language is allowable. This is, after all, your home. And, er, what do you call this place?" he asked, glancing again to the paradoxically fruitful tree.

"I just call it home. Or the tower." She shrugged, ladling out another bowl of broth.

"The tower. This is Ravenwood Tower. The Wizard's tower?"

"It is."

"Please, miss . . . Jade . . . Miss Jade! Fetch me my clothes, fetch me my weapons! We are both in grave danger--" he urged.

"Now, now, now. Either you lay back down or I'll have to put you to sleep," she warned, thrusting the bowl into his hands.

"Please. I came here to kill a terrible sorceress and her dragon. I've already defeated the beast, now--"

"That is just a lie."

"I assure you. There was a dragon, and I--"

"Oh, there was a dragon. You didn't kill him."

"I succumbed to my wounds, but the dragon must have done so as well, or surely I would not be here speaking to you. It would have killed me."

"Hal!"

"There is a man about? Excellent. He can help me get you to . . ."

The thundering of the dragon's approach silenced the prince. When Halfax emerged from the trees, the injured man leaped from the bed, hurled the soup messily to the floor, and threw himself in front of Jade.

"Go! Take shelter. I'll hold him as long as I can!" He proclaimed.

Halfax leaned low, looking through the doorway and focusing on the prince. The man's eyes flicked about the room until he spotted a knife on the table. He snatched the weapon and held it ready. The moment his fingers touched the blade, Halfax drew his lips back and rumbled a savage growl.

"Go!" Lumineblade cried, standing firm.

Man and beast were locked in each other's gaze. Slowly, Jade walked between them clutching a large, worn robe.

"Cover yourself, Terry," she said with a smirk. "And, Halfax, step out of the doorway, please. You seem to make Terry nervous."

With a final, vicious glare, he stepped aside. His shadow still hung threateningly across the walkway. Terrilius shakily donned the robe, awkwardly doing so without setting down the knife.

"The beast obeys you," he said in a hushed tone.

"I wouldn't call him obedient, but he's obliging if I'm reasonable. That is the dragon you attacked, right?"

"You . . . You're the sorceress. This is your tower."

"Sorceress? I've cast a spell or two, but . . ."

Before she could finish her thought the prince had bolted for the door, hobbling with remarkable speed out of the cottage and into the icy forest. Jade paced outside and crossed her arms, leaning against Halfax as she watched the injured man disappear into the woods.

"What a strange fellow. Brave, though. Standing up to you when he thought you might hurt me. Very brave."

"He is a fool," Halfax growled.

"No one said he can't be both."

#

The rush of intensity carried Terrilius deep into Ravenwood before it wore thin. When it did, it left him barefoot in an unfamiliar forest, clothed only in a robe, and armed only with a small knife. A dozen wounds throbbed, and the frozen air burned at his lungs, but still he willed himself forward. It wasn't fear or duty or even survival that drove him. He simply didn't know what else to do, and he had to do something. His pace dropped from a limping sprint to a painful trudge, and before long to a crawl to spare his freezing feet.

His plan had been to retreat, regroup, and retry. At the time, it had seemed obvious and natural. Now he was aware of a number of critical flaws in his plan. He had no men to regroup with, nowhere to retreat to, and no means to retry. The thought that he might die had never occurred to him. Not when he fought the dragon, not when he realized the nature of his host, and not now. His only concern was that he could not succeed at his task. A prince did not freeze. A prince did not fall in battle to a dragon. The only fear was disgrace, failure.

There was the crunch of footsteps. Slowly, he turned to see a pair of feet standing beside him. A moment later, his boots dropped on the ground in front of him. He looked up to see Jade, a blanket under one arm and a steaming flask in one hand.

"Ready to stop acting like a fool?" she asked.

"Where is your dragon?" he asked.

She shook her head and grinned. "My dragon. I asked him to wait back at the tower. I know he makes you nervous."

"H-how do I know I can trust you?"

"What could I possibly do to you that you haven't already done to yourself? If I wanted to kill you, I could have left you the way I found you and let nature take its course."

"Y-you could b-be trying to bewitch m-me."

"Well, then. Your options are to potentially be bewitched or certainly freeze to death. Would you like a moment to decide?" she asked, holding out a hand.

After a few more painful breaths, he took her hand and pulled himself up. Jade brushed the snow from him, wrapped him in the blanket, and handed him the flask.

"Now," she said, leading him to a fallen log, "we are going to have a seat, you are going to put your boots on, you are going to warm up, and you are going to tell me what all of this is about. Depending on what I hear, I may take you back and fix all of the damage you've done to yourself. Again."

It was a curious tone she used as she spoke. She didn't seem to be ordering him about. Rather, she was simply informing him of what would happen. The prince nodded numbly, dropping the knife to wrap both hands around the mercifully warm flask. It contained more of the broth, and the warmth that spread through him as he drank was revitalizing. When the chill finally left his voice, he spoke.

"I am the prince."

"That much I'd gathered."

"My father is a good man, but . . . he doesn't rule wisely. He feels it is his duty to keep his people safe, but the only threat he understands is invasion. He thinks a strong army is all he needs. But there are other problems. Disease. Hunger. He ignores them. I know that I can do better, that I can find ways to protect against all of these things, or at least try. When I become king, I will find a way . . . but . . . I have always known I am not respected. Always felt it.

I ask questions, I listen. That isn't what princes do, and certainly not what kings do. They act!

"Still, I didn't think it mattered. When I am king, they will *have* to respect me. But a man came to me and told me what people really thought . . . and that there were others who would take my throne away if they could. I knew that he was speaking the truth. I've seen them, and I know that my father thinks more highly of they than me. If I want to claim the throne I believe is my birthright, I knew that I would have to do something to earn their respect. He spoke of the sorceress and dragon . . . you, and your beast."

"His name is Halfax."

"Halfax. For three years, hunting much deeper than the fringe of Ravenwood has been forbidden in order to keep people safe from . . . you. If I could lead a mission to take the forest back, surely I would have their respect again."

The prince felt a sense of relief in telling his tale, as though a weight had been lifted from his shoulders. Voicing his fears or doubts to anyone in the palace would only make him seem weaker, but for some reason he felt comfortable telling them to Jade. None of this felt real to him. It was like confessing in a dream.

Jade nodded, adding, "Well, that explains a lot. It doesn't justify anything, but it explains plenty. So what are your plans now?"

"I . . . don't know. You are not what I had expected. But I can't let my people live in fear of you any more. I need to reclaim the forest. I can't go back without doing so."

Terrilius glanced about for a moment, his eyes coming to rest upon the knife where he had dropped it. He then looked to the eyes of his host. She didn't even have the courtesy to look nervous.

"You trust me not to hurt you? Knowing what I've told you?"

She chuckled.

"You were half dead when Halfax brought you in, and if you were to so much as look at me the wrong way, he would have a hard time keeping himself from finishing the job. Let's just say I'm not worried."

"But you said you asked him to stay behind."

"I did, and yet . . ."

She turned, prompting him to do the same. Looming over them, nearly close enough to touch them, was Halfax. The prince nearly leaped out of his skin, a firm hand from Jade the only thing that kept him from falling to the ground.

"I told you he wasn't obedient."

"But--how could he--I didn't hear a thing!"

"He's rather stealthy when he wants to be. Can you walk? Do you need help? I'd like to get you back to the tower and fix the stitches on your leg before you stain my robe too badly."

He made his way unsteadily to his feet, relying more than he cared to admit on the steady arm of his host as he did. The pair then made their way slowly back to the tower, Halfax following ominously behind.

#

"Here, drink this, it will help with the pain," Jade said when they reached her home.

"That is not necessary," he assured her.

"It isn't necessary because the one I poured down your throat while you were unconscious hasn't quite worn off yet. It will soon, and I'm about to run this through your leg a few times," she said, holding up a needle.

With what little dignity he could salvage, the prince took the cup and drained its contents. Almost as soon as the last drop was swallowed, the pain from his many wounds faded to little more than a dull ache. When she went to work with her needle, he was aware of it as a distant prickling sensation.

"Your magical skill is remarkable, sorceress," the prince said, "I am glad to know that your talents can be used for good as well as evil."

Jade stopped and narrowed her eyes at him briefly before resuming her task.

"First, I haven't cast any spells on you, and I don't intend to," she said as she worked. "That is a potion, so I wouldn't be a sorceress, I'd be an alchemist. Second, I've only cast perhaps five spells in my life. I would hardly call that a mastery of sorcery."

"But you control the dragon! Do not dare suggest that you trained this beast to behave as it does."

"Well, you're right about the training. The only things I ever taught him were how to cook and how to tend a garden. Most of the training went in the other direction."

"I don't understand."

"He raised me, Terry. Right here in this very tower, ever since I was six years old. Which reminds me. If you really thought he and I were so dangerous, why did you wait until three years ago to put a stop to all of the hunting?"

"Do not try to fool me. It was three years ago that you came to this place. Hundreds of my people witnessed you soaring overhead on the back of your beast, and you brought with you a storm impossibly brief and impossibly potent."

"Listen, I am telling you, I have lived here for twelve years! You can ask the people of Rook, they know me there. And besides, the last storm was--oh. Oh, I understand."

"What?"

"You'll see in a bit. Feet!" she said, sitting in a chair before him and patting her lap.

He automatically raised his feet and put them on her lap. It wasn't until she was halfway through unlacing his boots that he paused to question why she had asked for his feet--or, for that matter, why he had given them. It was something in the way she spoke, the way she seemed to assume she would have cooperation when she asked for it. Or perhaps it was the way she seemed to be so comfortable, so at ease in what she was doing. One simply felt obliged to obey. Terrilius told himself that it must be magic, but somehow it felt . . . natural.

"What are you doing?"

"You were running around in a frozen forest with your bare feet while under the effects of a pain-dulling potion. Between frostbite and jagged ice, I would like to make sure you still have all of your toes," she explained.

His feet were indeed a sorry sight, but a few dabs of medicine and a few bandages set them right again.

"Good, now get dressed. I'll show you what you came here to find," Jade said, handing to the still robe-clad prince the stained clothing he had been wearing beneath his armor.

"I--you--well, turn around, please," the prince replied.

With a grin, Jade turned until the prince was finished.

"All done? Follow me, and walk gently. I'm not sewing that leg up again."

Jade walked with the prince in tow for several minutes. There were a dozen things that should have been occupying the mind of the young nobleman. He should have been thinking about what she was bringing him to see, or perhaps what other things she might have done to him in the course of healing him.

Terrilius's mind, though, was firmly and unshakably focused on the woman before him. She was gorgeous, certainly, but there was no shortage of beauty in the castle. Likewise she was intelligent, and indeed there was not nearly enough of that. To the prince, the most impressive facet of Jade was her attitude. She had an honesty and confidence that he simply had never encountered before. The other nobles, the servants, the diplomats . . . they all behaved the same way. They spoke to the title, not to the man. A veneer of respect over a sea of contempt was the attitude he had come to expect from others. This woman, regardless of everything else, spoke to him as an individual. He wasn't Prince Terrilius. He was Terry. It was unsettling, disorienting, and fascinating.

They approached a clearing that resembled the remains of a dismantled lumber camp. The jagged, half-rotten stumps of trees that looked like they had been snapped off jutted from the ground. A mound of snow-covered rubble lay at one end of the clearing. For the most part, the place was dominated by a shallow black crater of charred earth. The air carried a vague but stinging odor, like burnt flesh and strong acid. There was a different quality to the cold as well. Something about it cut deeper here, creeping its icy fingers up the spine and into the mind.

"This is where it happened. Three years ago. A woman came. I don't know where she came from or what sent her, but she was certainly a sorceress. It must have been she who your people had seen," Jade said, with a shiver that had nothing to do with the cold, "That was a terrible day. I remember it so well. It was all Halfax could do to defeat her, and it almost cost him his life. That's what gave him the scar. That's what ruined his wings."

Terrilius looked into the crater as she continued.

"Three years . . . and snow still refuses to fall where she died. She rode in on this . . . thing," the young woman continued, walking over to the pile of rubble and brushing aside enough snow to reveal a skull-like head. "Halfax calls it a dragoyle. Nasty thing, but not nearly as nasty as her."

The prince looked over the decayed creature. The thought crossed his mind that she could be lying, but . . . the evil in this place was unmistakable. It hung in the air, pressing in on the mind like an oppressive heat. He didn't feel so much as a hint of the same from Jade. If this was what remained of a true evil sorceress, and it could be nothing else, then the woman beside him was nothing of the sort.

"If you came to defeat her, your job was done for you long ago."

"So it would seem . . ."

"You honestly came here hoping to defeat those two just to prove yourself worthy for the throne?"

"I did, and to restore the use of the forest to my people. Now it isn't to be."

"Well, the woods are yours. Ravenwood is massive. I didn't run into any hunters or the like in the years prior to your father's denial of access. I see no reason why anything would change."

"That is a blessing for my people, but it will do nothing for my standing among my peers," Terrilius said woefully.

Jade looked to the prince's down-turned mouth. He didn't *seem* angry or disappointed. Not once had he even lashed out about Halfax attacking him. There was nothing in his expression but regret and failure. He wanted glory, but not for any of the reasons that men normally sought it. To him it was a currency, a means to achieve what he felt he must.

"I am sorry to have disturbed you in this place. And I am sorry to have accused you. I will leave you to your tower, and I thank you on behalf of my kingdom for your aid."

"You aren't going anywhere just yet," Jade replied.

"I don't understand. I feel well enough."

"Again, only so long as the painkiller lasts, and I'm afraid you won't be getting another. It helps during treatment, but it slows the healing. When it wears off, I've got to administer something to speed the healing or I guarantee that one of those open wounds is going to take a turn for the worse, and in your state I doubt you'd survive it. In a few hours, you are going to become keenly aware of how many of your ribs Halfax managed to break, and how close he came to doing the same to your right arm."

"I must return to the castle."

"You will, but even with the help of healing potions, it is going to be at least another day before I feel you are ready to be bopping along on the back of a horse without rattling your bones apart again," she said.

"Men will come looking for me."

"Good. It will save us the trouble of tracking down your horse. Come on, back to the tower," she said, placing a hand upon his shoulder.

The short journey back to the tower was a quiet one. Terrilius had a look of despair that tugged at Jade's heart.

"Look, for three years everyone took it for granted that there was an evil sorceress in the forest. No one, not even the others vying for the crown, tried to confront her until you did. That has to be worth something," she offered.

"Spare me your sympathy, Miss Jade. I appreciate the kindness, but it simply isn't necessary. Is there anything I can do to aid my recovery?"

"As little as possible. When we get back to the tower, you should just lie down and rest. The treatments are going to be taxing your body's resources fairly heavily, and you'll be feeling it soon. You are in for a rough few days."

When they reached the tower once more, she laid him down on the cot and began issuing orders.

"Sleep if you can. There's broth in the pot and a bowl on the table. Eat if you're hungry. In fact, eat even if you aren't hungry. Healing up those breaks and tears in days instead of weeks is going to take every drop of raw material you can muster, so try to keep your belly full. I'll be tending to the garden and some other chores. Yell if you need me . . . and don't touch anything."

Terrilius lay upon the cot and gazed out the window at the snowy forest. As thoughts of failure and sorrow swirled in his mind, he squinted at the shadows between the trees. Just visible was the form of Halfax. Watching. With that chilling reality sitting heavily among the churning thoughts, he tried to get to sleep.

Chapter 10

It was hours before Jade offered more than a glimpse indoors to check on her patient. She was unaccustomed to company, and thus left something to be desired as a hostess. The sun was setting when she was through for the day. Her first stop was the pot of broth. Nearly empty.

"At least he follows orders," she muttered to herself.

She turned to the cot. He was lying where she had left him, but one look was all it took to know that sleep was not in his future. Sweat dripped from his forehead and drenched his clothes. His fists were clenched so tight they trembled, and his face bore a look of iron-hard concentration. The pain had returned, and it was clearly all he could do to bear it. She placed a hand upon his forehead. It was burning again. This was to be expected. His injuries had been severe, and while the things she had learned allowed her to work wonders, those wonders came at a cost.

"I'd like to tell you the worst is over, but . . . there is more on the way. Much more. Try to imagine it as all of the pain and suffering you would have felt over the normal healing process, but compressed into just a few hours. It is going to be an ordeal."

His only reply was the quick, short hiss of his breathing.

"Listen, you need to try to focus on something else. If you don't distract yourself, it will seem a thousand times worse."

He turned his bloodshot eyes to her before shutting them again.

"Here," she said, taking his hand and holding it tightly, "I'm right here. Talk to me. Was it worth it? Knowing how you feel now, and knowing that the sorceress and her beast would have left you in an even worse state, do you still feel like you needed to do this?"

"Yes, it was worth it! Even to try!" he growled through the pain.

"Really? Why?"

"Because a king needs to be more than a general! A king needs to care about more than borders. He . . . he sees Tressor and . . . they have an army. A massive one. They are not threatening, not moving, but . . . he sees an army, and he thinks the only way he can be safe is to have a bigger one. But we can't! We don't have the population for that! They will always have a bigger army. And when we begin massing troops, Kenvard and Ulvard start building up troops. It is dangerous! Unnecessary! There are better ways!"

His words were wild, passionate. They flew forth, propelled by pain and frustration and by the pressure of being held back for so long. Once spoken, though, the intensity quickly began to drain from his eyes and his mind began to wrap itself tightly about the pain again.

"Keep going. You have a better way? You would do it differently if you were king?"

"I . . . I . . . of course!" he said, grasping her hand in his. "Kingdoms don't go to war for no reason. They need things! Tressor has plenty of food, but barely any mines and very few forests. Vulcrest straddles the Rachis Mountains. We . . . everything you pull out of a mountain, we have to spare! But we have so little farmland."

"And?"

"We should give them copper, iron, coal. In return . . . they give us grain. Now . . . we need them. They need us. We don't need to try to match their army, because they can't afford to attack us and lose the trade!"

"That's . . . that's brilliant. Keep going! What else?"

For hours, through the worst of the pain, Terrilius spoke of the woes of his land and the solutions he envisioned. Some were flawed, others were inspired. Many were sweeping, revolutionary changes. They surely would require the full power of the throne to apply--but, in light of the troubles he described, they seemed nothing short of necessary. Widespread hunger, devastating disease outbreaks . . . all manner of problems plagued his people.

Jade had lived in this paradise for so long, and with her skills had helped to ease the suffering of the town of Rook so much, that she had forgotten the sorry state of the world that she had left behind. She'd managed to convince herself that things could not be as bad as she remembered. But to hear him speak of it, they were far worse.

Finally the pain crested and began to recede. Jade sat beside him and continued to hold his hand for more than an hour after exhaustion finally claimed him. He spoke with such dedication, such drive. It was unlike anyone she'd met, except perhaps Halfax. There was a spirit, a life to him when he spoke of those things he truly cared about. It made her care, too. For the first time since had she begged Halfax to take her to this place, Jade cared about the world outside of the niche she'd carved for herself. She wished he was awake again, so that he could hear him speak more of his kingdom and beyond . . . or simply just to hear him speak . . .

Throughout the night, Halfax had watched. Just because the boy was of a protected bloodline did not mean that the dragon trusted him. The prince had been planning to kill her, after all. His change of heart upon learning the truth could be an act. It was for this reason, the beast told himself, that he must watch. Deep inside though, far closer to his heart than he would ever allow himself to admit, there was another reason. He'd watched many generations of humans from afar. He knew the signs, the patterns. The way that she was looking at him, and he at her even through the pain, was familiar. He had seen many families begin with the same look. It was something that had been a long time coming. Something well past due. It was a sign that Jade would soon be ready to return to her own kind, to live the life that she deserved. It should have been what he was waiting for, what he wanted . . .

But he didn't want it now. Not *now*. In his heart, he wasn't ready.

For a dragon, everything is fleeting. Decades of memories blur together in the same way that days blur into each other for humans. Anything that takes less than a hundred years may as well be a blink of the eye. These twelve years . . . twelve short years . . . He never would have chosen this life for himself. He'd resisted it, planned constantly for the time when it would mercifully come to an end. But it had become comfortable. He had felt things he had never expected. Pride at watching her grow and learn. Fulfillment in teaching and protecting her. Happiness . . .

He dug his claws deeper into the ground. No. This was right. This was good. She would move on, as she should have years ago. It was as it should be. The rest didn't matter.

#

Terrilius woke the next afternoon to a ravenous hunger, a dull ache over his entire body, and the desire to sleep for another day. In a chair beside the cot was Jade. She was fast asleep, a book open upon her chest. He rose from the cot slowly, every joint in his body clicking and popping from lack of use. He managed to make it to his feet, but dizziness forced him to the cot again. Beside him was a pitcher of cool water and some coarse bread and dry meat. Hardly the courtly breakfast he was accustomed to, but at the moment his stomach assured him that it would do. He was stuffing his mouth in a distinctly unregal manner when his host awoke.

"Oh, oh, you're awake," she said, the residue of sleep slurring her words somewhat.

She closed the book and placed it on the table before standing and leaning over him. Rather than interrupting him, or even asking him, she began to test this part of his body and that, nodding thoughtfully as she did. A poke at the ribs, a squeeze at a shoulder and knee, and various gentle tests later, she spoke.

"No more bleeding, that's good. Still a bit swollen. Still a bit bruised. The breaks are almost finished knitting. That rapid healing treatment is really something, isn't it? How do you feel?" she asked. "Besides hungry."

"Tired. And sore."

"Your fingers look to be working just fine. I was a bit worried about your jaw, but if you can chew that stuff, you're fine. Move your feet a bit, would you? Yes. Yes, it looks like the potions did their work. A few aches when the weather is bad will be your only reminder of this little adventure."

Terrilius swallowed the last of the meat and water.

"I thank you for your aid, and, again, I apologize for my foolishness. If you can lend me a horse, I will be on my way to the castle."

"I don't have a horse. When I need to go somewhere, I ride Hal."

"Well, then I . . ."

He paused at the sound of rapidly retreating footsteps on the snow. Outside the window, he caught the merest glimpse of Halfax disappearing among the trees.

"Where is he off to?"

"Probably to find you a horse. I rather think Halfax is eager to be rid of you."

"He tried to kill me."

"You and your men tried to kill him, and planned to kill me. You can't fault Halfax for doing a better job. Besides, he brought you to me to fix you up, so that should set things right."

"I hardly think that it does . . . but it doesn't matter. It probably would have been better for my kingdom if he *had* killed me. This fiasco only proves how worthless I really am."

"Now, Terry, that's not true."

"It is! The very fact that I am still in this place is proof enough that my own men despise me. In the past, wars have been fought to secure the land where a royal had fallen. For me, they are unwilling to face a single dragon. But I do not blame them. What reason have I given them to respect me?"

"Precisely!" Jade snapped angrily, "What reason *have* you given them to respect you? For heaven's sake, Terry, you are a prince! Have some self-worth! I've only known you for two days, but in that time I've learned an awful lot about you. I've learned that you have ideas, good ones. I've learned that you've got more drive than a dozen men when you find something you care about. And yet somehow you think that none of that is enough to be a leader. How can you expect people to respect you if you don't respect yourself!?"

"I have done nothing of any worth in my life."

"Nothing? For three years, your father thought there was a terrible sorceress and her terrible dragon in this very tower. Who was the first one in all of that time to try to do something about it? You! You were doing it to prove you were a man worthy to lead, but anyone willing to risk it all for something they believe in is already worthy to lead. And you faced a dragon and lived to tell about it! I was going to fix up your scars, but--"

She smashed a vial on the floor, filling the room with a sharp scent.

"--to hell with it! You want people to respect you? You wear those scars like a trophy! And if that doesn't work, you come back here and you drag the head of that black dragon *thing* from the ground and give them a *real* trophy! You can lie and tell them you killed it with your bare hands and they will never know, but it won't matter, because they will never truly believe in you until you stand up straight and give them someone to believe in!"

Jade was out of breath, eyes wide and mind slowly catching up with what it had allowed to slip from her lips.

"Do you really--" he began.

His thought was cut short by approaching hoofbeats. A horse burst into the clearing. Not just any horse, but the very one that the prince had been knocked from when he first encountered the dragon. Halfax stalked in the shadows, his very presence enough to keep the frightened steed within the clearing that so few animals would venture into.

"Go! Get on your horse, go back to your people, and be the man you know you can be!" she demanded, pointing out the door.

The prince looked her in the eye, then looked to his horse. When his gaze returned to her, there was a look of resolve in his eyes. Without another word, he left the tower and climbed atop the horse. Halfax was nowhere to be found, vanished in order to permit the prince to leave. And so he rode off.

The dragon appeared again when the sound of hooves faded into the distance. He watched as Jade stood in the doorway, her eyes straining to watch the strange visitor leave. He knew from the look in her eye that her heart and mind went with him.

#

If there had been any doubt that the young man had made an impression upon her, the days that followed put it to rest. She spoke only of "Terry." She told of the ideas he'd had, of the remarkably swift recovery. Sometimes she spoke of things that irritated her, other times of things she had admired, but always she spoke of him.

Halfax weathered the constant conversation with his usual stoicism, but beneath the surface, his emotions churned. Anger, resentment, and acceptance clashed within him at the mention of the prince's name. Those tossed about upon a sea of emotion often become adept at concealing them. The dragon, his feelings usually so subdued, was unaccustomed to such things. It was weeks later. as he and Jade strolled leisurely side by side, returning from one of their frequent trips to forage for herbs, that the young woman finally spoke up.

"Is something wrong?" she asked, stooping to pluck a sprig from between two stones.

"No."

"You seem distant. More so than usual."

"There is nothing wrong," he rumbled.

"Clearly. Well, you are certainly acting differently. Ever since you brought Terry."

The dragon released a brief, involuntary growl at the sound of the name.

"I thought so. Are you still angry at him? You and I both know it was a simple misunderstanding when he wanted to kill me."

"It doesn't matter."

"You don't feel bad about hurting him, do you? He made a full recovery, and he did everything to deserve it. There is nothing to feel guilty about."

"I do *not* feel guilty."

"Then why act this way? It isn't as though . . . Hal?"

The dragon had stopped, eyes suddenly locked on the tower between the trees in the distance.

"What is it, Hal?"

"He is here."

"Terry?" she asked, a heavy dose of excitement in her voice tempered with a dash of confusion.

"He is in the tower."

Jade squinted into the distance and could just make out the form of a horse standing uneasily outside the ring of good weather. She took a few dozen steps toward the tower, fairly giddy with the prospect of another visit, but stopped when she realized that Halfax was not following.

"Well? Aren't you coming?"

"It would be best if I kept my distance."

"Humph. Suit yourself," she said, quickly continuing on her way.

At the sound of her approach, Terrilius appeared at the doorway.

"Terry!" She said with a wide smile.

"Hello, Miss Jade, I . . ." he began, holding out a hand to take hers in a courtly greeting.

She pushed the gesture aside in favor of a hug that seemed to make the prince every bit as uncomfortable as it did the dragon.

"What brings you back to the tower?" she asked, bringing him inside and sitting him down.

"I wished to thank you."

"Oh, no thanks needed, Terry. You were in bad shape when you came here last. I couldn't very well leave you to die . . . though I was tempted, looking at what your men did to Hal."

"Er, yes. Of course, I am quite grateful for that, but you did more for me that day than repair my body."

"I don't think I did . . ." she said doubtfully.

"I encountered some of my own men as I left the tower. It was a small search party that was afraid to venture near to where your dragon was encountered. The sight of me alive, and with the scars, after what the others had told of the beast's attack . . ."

"Defense, you mean."

"Yes, defense. Well, my survival did wonders for my reputation. When I returned to castle, I began to think of what you'd said. About my ideas. About confidence. You lit a fire in me that day. I said my piece, and my father . . . listened. Already I can sense a difference in the way I am treated, in the way that I am seen. It is thanks to you and your advice."

"No, no, no. I didn't do anything but tell you what you should have already known."

"So you say, but how could *you* have known? You and I had met only a day prior, and you revealed to me things about myself that even I didn't know."

"Well, I've spent more than a few nights by the bedside. Pain, disease. They strip away a few layers. Let you see what's underneath. There is a lot to see."

"Well, in light of your help in saving my life and my future, I wish to reward you," he said, pulling open a large sack.

"Entirely unnecessar--is that a full moon herb? And a telra root?"

She reached into the bag and rummaged around.

"Powdered lapis! Dried cutleaf!" She exclaimed as she pulled each from the bag.

"We haven't a single scholar who knows a thing about potions and magics as you do, but these were a few rare substances my advisers tell me were valued by the mystics of the past."

"You have no idea the good I can do with some of this. Do you have a source for these ingredients? Can you give me a name? With a ready supply, I could--"

"If they are useful to you, I shall see that you have more than you shall ever need. But I did not come here only to give you gifts."

"I imagine you'll want your armor back, too."

"Well, yes, but I had hoped, perhaps, you might share with me some more of your insight."

"About what?"

"My father has agreed to attempt to open trade with Tressor, but there is much to consider. I could think of no one whose thoughts I would value more highly than yours."

"Of course I'll help, Terry!"

#

And so it began. He stayed for two days, and in that time, they discussed everything from royal diplomacy to the methods Jade used to keep her garden so healthy. Not a month later, he had returned again, with bags of gifts and a head full of questions. The visits became a regular occurrence, which Jade eagerly looked forward to.

With each appearance, and with each discussion, the tone of their interactions subtly changed. Jade asked questions of the prince now. She asked about the places she'd read of in her books. She asked of other lands, of great festivals. Tales of life in the castle fascinated her. As they spoke they smiled and laughed. And all the while, Halfax watched from afar.

Again, the dragon was no stranger to the ways of humans. His duty in protecting generation after generation of humans had seen him bear witness to dozens of flowering relationships. She had feelings for him, and he for her. It was in their eyes, in the tone of their voice, in their posture, even their scent. Each time they spoke, Jade seemed more interested in his tales of the capital, and Terrilius more insistent that she become an official adviser.

Thus, when the prince approached one day not upon a horse but inexpertly leading a carriage, Halfax knew precisely the reason why.

Chapter 11

There was no true road to Jade's tower. It hadn't been a problem when the prince had come by horseback, but navigating even the small carriage between the trees and over the rough ground was no small task. Terrilius struggled with the reins and quietly cursed his inability to find a willing driver. Despite his many trips to the tower and back, none of his soldiers or his servants were ever willing to accompany him, so great was their fear of Halfax and so stubborn their distaste for the man he had been. It was fortunate in that it provided the prince with a measure of privacy for his meetings with Jade, but it meant that he was left to guide the carriage with his own hand.

Suddenly, the horse, increasingly hesitant as they traveled, faltered and refused to go any further. There was little doubt as to why.

"You know that I mean her no harm, dragon," he spoke aloud, trying to keep his voice from shaking.

The prince's eyes were wide, sweeping the shadows that suddenly seemed so dark and numerous.

"You have kept your distance since that day, dragon. A wise decision. Why stop me now?"

"Because until now, you brought things with you. Today you mean to take something away," the beast replied.

His voice was a rattling growl, deep and resounding, and powerful enough to shake little cascades of snow from the trees. It was the first time the young man had heard Halfax speak, and it chilled him to the bone. Terrilius drew his weapon, a well-made and pristine short sword, and tried to steady himself once more.

"Jade is coming with me," the prince stated, sword held low but ready.

"Yes. She is," Halfax rumbled.

Like lightning, his tail lashed forward, striking the sword and whipping it away. When it was well out of reach, he slid from the shadows, eyes locked on the young man.

"She is going with you. Not because it is what you want. Because it is what she wants."

"And you will allow her?"

"It is not my place to allow her or disallow her. She does as she wishes. Her life is her own, to live as she sees fit. And she wants to be with you.

"But know this. I will *never* be far from her. I will *always* be watching. If you ever hurt her, if you ever fail her, if you allow even a single tear to run down her cheek . . . there is nowhere you can go that I can't follow. There is nowhere you can hide that I can't find you. And when I do, there won't be enough of you left to bury."

He stepped forward until his snout was inches from the prince's face, smoldering breath nearly singeing the boy's hair.

"They won't even find your bones."

With those ominous words, Halfax slipped back into the shadows. Moments later, though there had been not a whisper of sound, the dragon was gone. The carriage continued on its way, reaching the tower not long after. The prince entered, and from his place in the forest, Halfax watched. He watched Jade's eyes light up at the sight of him. He watched her consider the noble's words and he watched her, with a joyful embrace, accept.

"Hal!" Her voice rang out.

The dragon paced toward the tower, Terrilius leaving to ready the carriage. The two exchanged a tense look as they passed. Jade was standing in the doorway, her expression vaguely uncertain.

"What is it?" the beast asked.

"He wants me to go with him, Halfax," Jade said, something between excitement and anxiety in her voice.

"Do you want to go with him?" he asked.

"I do. I really do. I never realized how backward things were. It wasn't just my home village. It isn't just Rook. The whole world has turned its back on knowledge. I have so much to offer. I can help so many people. He wants to make me his head adviser . . . and . . . when the time comes . . . his queen. If I go with him, I can change things. The two of us can bring a little light back into the world. You and I can--"

"No."

"What? What do you mean *no?*"

"There cannot be you and I. Not anymore. Not if you go with him to the capital."

"Why not?"

"There is no place for me there."

"We can find a place for you! He has a palace!"

"A dragon does not belong in a city. The people would not allow it."

"He's the prince!" she exclaimed in rising desperation, tears beginning to flow. "He can order the guards to leave you alone. He can order the people to--"

"He cannot order them not to hate and fear me. He cannot order them not to see me as an enemy, and you as a traitor for bringing me. I cannot protect you if we are surrounded by terrified people. I'll watch over you, and if something threatens you, I will be there for you. But I cannot be by your side."

"Then . . . then I won't go! I'll find another way!"

"That isn't what you want."

"I want . . . I want you to be a part of my life, Halfax, I . . . I know I never said it, because I know how uncomfortable it makes you when I show you affection, but . . . I love you, Halfax. You are the closest thing I have to a father. You gave me shelter and food, and you raised me. Everything I am is because of you. I'm thankful for that, but you gave me something else that has meant so much more. You gave me you. You were my family when mine was taken away. I don't want to lose you like I lost them."

"You aren't losing me. I will always be watching you. You may not see me, but I will always be there."

"But . . . I . . ."

Jade looked Halfax hard in the eye. She didn't see anger there--or hatred, or malice. She saw instead acceptance, peace, and sorrow. He wasn't doing this to hurt her, because she was abandoning him. He was doing it because he believed it was right. Deep inside, she knew it was, too. It was time.

"So . . . back to normal for you, then. Lurking in the shadows, making sure nothing hurts me. Just like you've done for everyone before me." She sniffled, wiping away some tears and attempting a smile. "This must seem so silly for you. Me crying like a baby when you've had to do this so many times before."

"No. Never like this. Most of those before you didn't even know I was there. Those who did treated me like a curse, or a blessing. I was just a force in their lives. Each of them had been my burden. My responsibility. My duty. You are the only one who has simply been . . . mine."

For a moment, there were no more words. Jade stepped forward and embraced the dragon's neck. He clutched her lightly to him with his paw. When the moment was over, Jade stepped back and smiled through the tears once more.

"Well, I suppose that's it, then. They have a place for me in the palace. I don't suppose there is anything here I need to bring. I'll leave my things. If you ever end up with another stubborn brat like me, at least they'll have something to read."

She sniffled again, and began to walk toward the small carriage the prince had waiting.

"I'll miss your cooking!" she called back to him. "And don't think I've forgotten about your wings! I'll keep searching for something to fix them, and if I find it, I'll track you down whether you like it or not!"

She climbed into the carriage and turned back. The dragon was gone.

"Goodbye . . ." she whispered.

The carriage creaked off into the distance. When it was out of sight, Halfax slipped from the shadows. He took a few steps toward the stable, his eyes on the handful of coins that made up his hoard. Standing over them, his eyes turned to the distant sound of the carriage. He touched a claw to the crudely engraved amulet that hung about his neck. A moment later he was on their trail, carefully out of sight, the coins left behind.

#

An aging man sat alone at a table in the town of Isintist. His mind drifted back to years ago. It had all seemed to be turning around then, it--

"It all seemed to be going your way," a voice uttered, finishing his thought, "didn't it, Mr. Drudder?"

The man's head snapped around to see a face from his past he'd hoped never to see again. It was the elf. Thanks to his kind's frustrating freedom from the ravages of age, the scoundrel didn't look a day older. He could have stepped straight from Drudder's memory.

"What are you doing here!?"

"Plans often go awry, Mr. Drudder. I, for instance, have had an irritating number of schemes fail of late. For instance, do you remember Jade? The little girl I suggested that you pitch to the dragon?"

"Y-yeah."

"The plan was for her to die. Just as her family died when you, in response to my own musings, touched a torch to her home."

"Yeah."

"I had my own reasons for wanting the lot of them dead, though, of course, it was you who performed the act. You see, Drudder, there are a number of very important families. Families descended from a handful of individuals I've had to deal with in the past. If I ever want to take another stab at what I was working toward back then, it would be immensely useful to end those families now. The Chosen bloodlines. There are only three left, and I've whittled each of them down to little more than a single representative. But these last ones . . . the dragon, the girl, and the prince . . . they *are* tenacious."

"What prince are--"

"Jade, for instance. Good heavens, is she a lucky one. Dodged the fire, naturally. I knew the dragon wouldn't kill her. Still, I genuinely thought that the classic scenario would play out. A damsel in distress under the watchful eye of a fearsome dragon. Egad, she even found her way into the highest room in the tallest tower. It should have brought the glory-hunters crawling out of the woodwork. A veritable *army* to slay that dragon. But it wasn't to be. The damned girl was just too lucky, and the damned dragon too good at his job. He was even too smart to kill *you*, even though you richly deserved it."

"The dragon didn't kill the girl!?" Drudder stammered, falling further and further behind the conversation.

"I tried the more direct approach, obviously. I armed someone, made a weapon of her, and I sent her off. It didn't work. I contemplated giving up then and there, but what can I say? I like a challenge. In situations like this, if you want to succeed, you need to be even *more* direct, put your own hands on the thing, or else find a different route to victory all together. So I threw the three

89

bloodlines together. And do you know what happened? That girl is going to be a *queen!* It seems like a failure on my part, doesn't it?"

"I don't understand!"

"But look at it from the bird's eye. There are three bloodlines now. When they are wed, there will be two. One less than before. I've eliminated a bloodline without killing any of them. I'm rather proud of that. So proud, in fact, that it has got me in a charitable mood. I'll let her have her happily ever after. Perhaps in a few generations I'll have another go, but she's earned a respite."

"Listen to me!" Drudder screamed, finally at wit's end, "I killed the Rintons and I killed that little girl for *me!* For the *land!* And that little girl, she was a *witch!* She *had* to die! I don't need you coming to me, after all of these years, and telling me I was doing it for *you!* That it was some insane plan! So if you are feeling so charitable, then why don't you leave me alone. Take your lies and get off of *my* land!"

The stranger grinned as his host tried to catch his breath, fury in his eyes.

"You idiot. I'm not feeling charitable to *you.* All *you* did was play the villain, and if Jade is to have the fairytale ending she so richly deserves, we can't very well allow the wicked stepfather to escape justice, now can we?"

Suddenly, the door to the house was kicked open. An ancient man, clinging to a walking stick to remain erect, stood surrounded by the strongest men the town had to offer. The muscle rushed into the room, restraining Drudder and the stranger. Delnick, the shriveled but still sharp-minded elder, stepped inside and stood face to wizened face.

"I always suspected you, Drudder. That Rinton house didn't just burn down all of those years ago," Delnick wheezed, "and in my town, we don't forget a murder."

"I didn't, I swear!"

"I'm half deaf, and even I heard you crying out your confession. I'm not a complicated man. I believe in simple punishments. You killed those folks. You and your elf here. So I figure it is long past time for you two to swing. Tonight!"

In the light of the moon, a man could already be seen through the doorway draping a rope over a branch outside.

"Why!? Why would you do this!? You'll be killed, too!" Drudder raved to the stranger as he was dragged outside.

"Death isn't as thorough a punishment for some as it is for others," he said calmly.

"Keep your mouth shut, stranger," Delnick warned.

"Please," he replied with a grin, "call me Epidime."

#

As Jade had suggested, life for Halfax returned to what it had been before he encountered Jade. The capital of Vulcrest was nestled among the mountains at the very northernmost point on the continent. Among the icy peaks were an

90

endless array of perches and alcoves. He settled himself into a cave, the same that had, at one time, been used by his brother before him, and stood vigilant in the cliffs around the castle. Hunting was scarce, but his skills were enough to keep himself fed. And so the days began to blend into weeks, months, and years.

There came prosperity, and peace. First as prince, then as king, Terrilius ushered in allegiance and partnership between nations. First as adviser, then as queen, Jade brought with her the teachings she had earned in the tower, and the dedication to show the world that knowledge was not to be feared but embraced. A long, dark age began finally to see dawn. The clouds of ignorance parted, and society began to take its first steps back into the light. True, as with all changes of the guard, it was not without incident. There were skirmishes, plots, and threats, but swift action by the royal guard--and, more than once, by Halfax himself--set things right again.

Things were as they should be. Each piece in its place.

#

"This will do," the queen said with a smile.

Queen Jade, while much beloved by her subjects, did have some quirks that puzzled the palace staff. In general, she did not allow her servants to serve. Many of the activities seen as well below the concern of a royal were cheerfully undertaken personally. She spent far more time in the kitchen, or the infirmary, or the freshly reestablished library than in the throne room. Now she had been asked to be brought to a remote, icy field far to the southwest of the palace with nary an explanation given.

It had been nearly ten years since she had left the tower and just a bit more than two since she had become Queen. The time had, if anything, made her more beautiful, bestowing upon Jade a grace and wisdom every bit the complement to her radiance. She flashed a smile to those servants who had accompanied her.

"You can head back to Tus Point tavern for a few hours."

"Which of us, your Majesty?" asked the most senior of her three escorts.

"All of you!" she said brightly, "I need a few hours to clear my head, and this is just the place to do it. Go, with my blessings, and enjoy yourselves. A few moments alone with my thoughts are all I'm after."

"Alone? But what if-"

"Don't make me order you. You know how I hate to do that," she said politely.

Reluctantly, she was left with her carriage while the driver, the guard, and the handmaiden shared two horses back to the town in the nearby valley. Jade watched them go. When they disappeared behind the hills at the edge of the field, she turned to the mountains. After a time, a form appeared and moved, fast and low to the ground, toward her. Despite the fact that it was a green shape moving against a white landscape, if she didn't keep her eyes carefully trained on it the form slipped quickly from notice. In no time at all, her old friend was standing before her.

"It has been too long, Hal," she said, hugging the creature, "Too, too long."

"You shouldn't do this. If people were to see . . ."

"Honestly, Hal, you make it sound like I'm having an affair," she said mischievously, "Besides, there is someone I want you to meet."

Jade turned to the carriage and opened the door. Carefully she turned back, clutching what appeared to be a small bundle of fine cloth. Gently she pulled aside a flap of cloth, revealing the tiny pink face of a baby girl, sleeping soundly in her mother's arms.

"I would have liked this to be a surprise, but I know you've been watching me all along, just as you said you would," she said softly, "I wanted to name her after you, but, well . . . Halfax as a girl's name, even for a princess . . . It wouldn't do. But then I thought back to that story. The one you used to tell when I couldn't sleep? The one about the Chosen that fought for this world . . . Halfax . . . Say hello to Myn."

"My mother? You named her for my mother?" he uttered, in a gentle a voice as he could muster.

Even with his great care, the dragon's voice woke the child. It sleepily opened its eyes and locked them on the beast. A tiny hand reached out, prompting Halfax to take a cautious step back. The baby smiled. Jade rocked her slowly in her arms until the little one's eyes closed again.

"It only seems right. All of those years ago, Myranda found a tiny defenseless creature and named it Myn. She kept it safe, taught it well. Then you did the same for me. Now it has come full circle," Jade said, looking at the face of the child.

She opened the door to the carriage and tucked the infant inside once more.

"When I was a little girl," she said, turning back to her friend, "I made you promise me that you would take care of me forever. Even though it was already your duty, I wanted you to make the promise to me personally. You've kept your word better than I could have imagined, but from this day forward, I relieve you of that promise. From now on, your obligation is to this little girl. I want you to watch over her, not just because it is your purpose, but for me."

"Of course . . ." he said, almost reverently.

And so the two shared their brief visit. It would not be the last. Terrilius and Jade's reign was a long and honored one. Knowledge and learning spread. An old era receded, a new one began. With each generation, the world crawled a little further from the fog of its past and into the bright day of its future. And with each generation Halfax watched, waiting for next time he would be needed. Waiting, and remembering the one little girl who had truly been his.

###

From The Author

Thank you for reading this story. The tale is set some time after another of my stories, the Book of Deacon Trilogy. If you enjoyed this book and would like to learn more about the history of its world, you might enjoy the trilogy as well. Whether you liked my work or not, I would love to hear what you think, so please leave a review. It will help me to improve the things that you didn't like, and to give you more of the things you did. And finally, if you'd like to hear about my latest projects, please sign up for my newsletter.

Discover other titles by Joseph R. Lallo:

The Book of Deacon Saga:
Book 1: *The Book of Deacon*
Book 2: *The Great Convergence*
Book 3: *The Battle of Verril*
Book 4: *The D'Karon Apprentice*

Book of Deacon Side Stories:
Jade
The Rise of the Red Shadow

The Big Sigma Series:
Book 1: *Bypass Gemini*
Book 2: *Unstable Prototypes*
Book 3: *Artificial Evolution*
Book 4: *Temporal Contingency*

NaNoWriMo Experiments:
The Other Eight
Free-Wrench
Skykeep

Connect with Joseph R. Lallo

Website: www.bookofdeacon.com
Twitter: @jrlallo
Tumblr: jrlallo.tumblr.com

www.ingramcontent.com/pod-product-compliance
Lightning Source LLC
Chambersburg PA
CBHW071009120726
47910CB00004B/1449